DISPUTED LAND

Also by Tim Pears

In the Place of Fallen Leaves
In a Land of Plenty
A Revolution of the Sun
Wake Up
Blenheim Orchard
Landed

Tim Pears

DISPUTED LAND

WILLIAM HEINEMANN: LONDON

Published by William Heinemann 2011

2 4 6 8 10 9 7 5 3

Copyright © Tim Pears 2011

First published in Great Britain in 2011 by
William Heinemann
Random House, 20 Vauxhall Bridge Road,
London SW1V 2SA

www.rbooks.co.uk

Addresses for companies within The Random House Group Limited can be found at:
www.randomhouse.co.uk/offices.htm

The Random House Group Limited Reg. No. 954009

A CIP catalogue record for this book
is available from the British Library

ISBN 9780434020812

The Random House Group Limited supports the Forest Stewardship Council® (FSC®),
the leading international forest certification organisation. All our titles that are printed on
Greenpeace approved FSC® certified paper carry the FSC® logo.
Our paper procurement policy can be found at www.randomhouse.co.uk/environment

For Hania

On Wenlock Edge the wood's in trouble
His forest fleece the Wrekin heaves;
The gale, it plies the saplings double,
And thick on Severn snow the leaves.

＊　＊　＊　＊　＊

The gale, it plies the saplings double,
It blows so hard, 'twill soon be gone:
Today the Roman and his trouble
Are ashes under Uricon.

from *A Shropshire Lad* by A. E. Housman

PROLOGUE

My son wondered why I had wanted to write down the following story. 'For posterity?' he asked. 'For the future? There is no future. There's only now.'

He knows the story, an episode from my childhood. He's heard the basic facts before.

'Is it for us?'

'Perhaps. Yes. For you, and for your children.'

This was a pat answer, and avoided the issues implied by my son's question. The futility of art, when action was needed. The absurdity of producing more, now. Writers have, I imagine, always asked themselves whether or not they would continue if they knew that no one would ever read what they were writing.

'I think it's for the people of whom I write,' I told him, the idea coming to me as I said it; having already written the first draft. It wasn't a conscious motive, or motivation, in the process of composition, but, having summoned the memories recalled in these pages, having resurrected time spent with these people, it seemed to me that I had done so for them.

'But most of them are gone,' my son said.

Perhaps, I thought, it is possible to produce something, now, not only for the future but also for the past. Perhaps in some way the story as I have written it, or my communion with the spirit of those members of my family, is not only a consolation for the passage of time but a call across it.

My son laughed. 'You mean,' he said, 'that those people, as

they were, fifty years ago, would receive some, I don't know, consoling, enlightening emanation from the future?'

'I don't know,' I admitted, 'what I mean.'

My son – and his brother and his sister – think it's vanity, or evasion, no kind of legacy compared to the real one that they and their own children have to deal with.

He thinks that I and my generation should have done more to slay the false gods of growth and greed. Where have they brought us? The cornucopia of food from my childhood is a decadent dream; fuel is ruinously expensive; yet, in comparison with most places on this earth, our island is a haven others make for. They scramble ashore and head inland.

And then it occurred to me that yes, I have indeed written it for you, my son. That this is the best way I can explain to you why it was we failed. Judge us as you will.

I

I

We trundled along. I sat alone in the back, listening on my Samsung MP3 player to Julian Bream playing *Danzas españolas* by Enrique Granados, which my mother had downloaded for me especially for the journey. The recording was old, and there was a little background hiss, but I didn't mind. To tell the truth, I rather liked that poor sound quality. It rendered the performance less Olympian, made it easier to imagine that I might one day play as well as that maestro, would coax such tonal range from my own acoustic guitar.

My father drove, my mother sat beside him in the front. The music, spare and delicate, with its dancing melody, building into a gorgeous powerful theme, played in my headphones while the dismal English countryside, with its dreary towns, sidled past.

I never answered the telephone in those days. There was no reason why I should. It was never for me. My own mobile only ever bleeped: my mother, usually, texting to save money, wondering where r u? As for the landline, they could answer it themselves. I wasn't my parents' servant. Their unpaid skivvy. Oh, sure, there'd been a time when I was happy to answer. I enjoyed doing so, I admit. 'This is the Cannon Duran residence. How can I help you?' I'd pass the receiver to whichever parent had been asked for, they'd listen for a moment and then Mum would say, 'Yes, he is a wonderful secretary, we couldn't ask for better.' Dad on the other hand would provide some wry aside like, 'We're grooming him for a job in a call centre.'

By now, at thirteen, I'd long grown out of that juvenile phase. The day before our journey, however, the phone rang while I was hanging around in the hallway.

'Get that, would you?' Mum called from the kitchen.

'Where's Dad?' I countered.

'Checking the car.'

'Checking what?' I yelled back. 'I could have told him it's still there.' The ringing tone grew louder.

'Tyres,' Mum shouted. 'Oil. I don't know. Will you just answer it?'

By now the machine had come on. My mother's calm voice stated, *Hello. This is the answerphone of Rodney Cannon, Amy Duran and Theo Cannon. Please leave a message after the tone.*

'Why don't *you* get it?' I wondered out loud.

'I'm up to my elbows in this gunk,' Mum wailed. '*Please,* Theo.'

After the tone had sounded there was a long, uncertain pause, before an imperious voice announced, 'It's me.' After a further delay, 'What time do you plan to arrive? I need to know whether or not I'm feeding you.'

What, I wondered, like penguins in a zoo? I picked up the receiver and said, 'Hello, Grandma.'

'Is that you, Rodney?'

'No, it's Theo, Grandma.'

'Oh,' she said, surprised, if not disappointed. 'How *are* you, darling?'

'Me?' I pondered. 'Well, I guess I'm sort of –'

'Never mind,' she interrupted. 'We'll catch up tomorrow. When are you going to get here?'

'After lunch, I suppose,' I said. 'We'll eat in the car as usual.' This was one of our family rituals: any drive over an hour long was timed, if possible, to include a packed lunch, a proven method, begun when I was small, of making a long journey bearable.

'You're coming by *car*?' Grandma exclaimed, apparently shocked by the prospect.

'Well, yeah,' I murmured. 'I mean, we always do.'

'Have you people not got the foggiest idea what's happening?' Grandma demanded. 'We've simply *got* to stop using these horrible combustion engines. All of us. Come by train. I'll have Jockie meet you at the station.'

The nearest railway station was miles away from my grandparents' house, I felt sure; in Ludlow or Craven Arms or one of those places. 'How would Jockie get between the village and the station?' I asked. 'He'd have to drive, wouldn't he?'

There was another pause. I feared Grandma was going to reprimand me for being impertinent. Instead, she said, 'We've not got rid of *all* the horses, Theo.'

We drove through the Cotswolds (thus avoiding the motorways, for 'aesthetic reasons', according to my father) at a steady fifty-five miles per hour on the open road, in order to conserve fuel, but also because this was the least stressful speed for a driver, as scientifically proven by the AA and the RAC, so Dad said. His own pulse rate, he claimed, rose exponentially with every increase in velocity from that point. He paid no attention to the suffering caused to the passenger in the rear seat, namely myself, by travelling at such a tedious speed. If I tried to read a magazine, however, I was likely to throw up in a plastic bag, a supply of which my mother kept in the glove compartment. I

5

found it curious – and not a little annoying – that my stomach could cope with sandwiches, crisps and apples chomped into it, but was turned by my eyes perusing a printed page; such, I concluded, were the mysterious frailties of the human organism.

Outside, a soft drizzle of rain fell from a grey, blotchy sky. The landscape was drained of colour. The wipers tick-tocked mournfully across the windscreen as we made our way to my grandparents' house for Christmas on Tuesday the twenty-third of December, two thousand and eight, in common no doubt with the occupants of all the other cars, vans, coaches and lorries that passed by or overtook us, criss-crossing the country, scuttling to and fro across the spider web of our intimate diasporas, our familial dispersals.

It was just as well my father drove so slowly. He did it not only for his own sake but also that of our car, a Morris Traveller built in 1970. It was twenty-five years older than I was. His profound attachment to that croaking old vehicle might have been seen as curious for a man who claimed not to understand how any mechanical device more recent or more complex than the Archimedean Screw functioned. 'And I don't really know how that works, to tell the truth,' he admitted. Actually, I knew more about Archimedes than my father did, from when we'd studied the Romans: Archimedes invented engines of war for the defence of Syracuse.

My father was clueless when it came to DIY, but he would happily spend hours of a summer evening sanding down, by hand, the Morris Traveller's distinctive exterior woodwork, and revarnishing it with loving strokes of a sable-haired paintbrush. I'd been with him a month earlier, when, after its annual MOT and service, he went to pick it up from the garage in Farndon Road, whose owner and sole mechanic had been tending my

6

father's car for the past thirty years. The two men stood in front of her, addressing each other formally: Mr Weaver explained that he'd put in an alternator conversion and new brake drums, and that he might need to take a look at the sills next year, but for now she still ran like a beauty, to all of which Dad nodded sagely; and I noticed that, possibly unbeknownst to either themselves or one another, each man had placed a hand on one of the rounded wings of the almond green chassis, and caressed the old girl with a tender appreciation.

Now, Julian Bream having brought his virtuoso performance to a close, I removed the headphones. My parents were gabbling away to each other in the front. Compared to the acoustically sealed environment of a modern automobile, our antique rattletrap made a racket, both its own noisy engine and the roar of the road. Since there was nothing my parents valued more than peace and quiet in which to babble at each other it was odd we had a car that forced them to raise their voices. They discussed the imminent closure of another post office in north Oxford, and the historically proven impossibility of an occupying army imposing peace in Afghanistan. Rolling through Stow-on-the-Wold and Upper Swell, my parents gossiped about their friends and criticised work colleagues. My father proclaimed that the only answer to the present credit crunch recession in Britain, 'the British solution', was for patriotic consumer-citizens to buy their way out, a proposal which annoyed my anti-materialist mother, who did not enjoy irony, but amused him enormously. I tried to ignore them, zoning in and out of their conversations as they pondered improvements to our house, following their recent coup of having our loft insulated for just one hundred and ninety eight pounds, 'materials *and* labour', my father reiterated, courtesy of a Tesco special offer; and my mother, despite our never having owned a family pet, ruminated upon whether our long, thin garden would be a more suitable environment for chickens or for bees.

The fact of the matter was that, wittering on at each other, my parents forgot I was there. I leaned against the side behind my father's head, out of his eyeline in the rear-view mirror. The car smelled old in a way I despised at the time, though now, as the smell of venerable leather returns in my memory as strongly as if in my very nostrils, I remember it only with an affection as fond as my father's. 'You may not appreciate her now, Theo,' he'd say, chuckling in the face of my teenage contempt. 'She'll likely be the major part of your inheritance.' If I have moved through life at the same speed as my father – if I tell stories at as leisurely a pace as he drove – then I can only apologise; though it could hardly be helped. Our legacies are limited.

We stopped in a lay-by with a roadside snack bar, outlets which, in Mum's opinion, tended to sell dreadful coffee but drinkable tea. My father turned to climb out of the car, and when he saw me he gave a little start, before saying with a smile, 'Theo. I forgot you were there.' He didn't mean it had slipped his mind that I was in the back of the car accompanying him and his wife, my mother, on this particular journey. What he really meant was that he'd forgotten that I, his son, his only child, existed. That Mum and he were not still going out together, as they had for many years before my birth. Their relationship was an endless, intermittent conversation which my unplanned arrival had interrupted. I could only imagine their relief when they discovered how easy it was to resume their conversation, and leave me to my own devices as I sat behind them. I'd not been joined by any brother or sister – for reasons as mysterious to my parents, probably, as my appearance had been. I wouldn't have been surprised if they'd only ever once had sex, considering what that worrisome prospect entailed.

Two men ran the snack bar. They had identical bull necks, thick square heads, close-cropped hair and pale blue eyes; they could have been father and son, or possibly brothers.

'What can I get you, chap?' the younger one asked Dad, who I could tell was a little disconcerted by this form of address. But he ordered three teas, and paid for them. We waited while the drinks were poured, the three of us, silenced by the periodical noise of the traffic thudding past.

'There you go, mate,' the older one said, placing our drinks on the counter.

We carried the hot styrofoam cups back to the car, got in, closed the doors. Mum turned and said, 'I'm sorry, Rod, all I'm saying is, don't blame me if I go into my shell. I just don't know how to deal with your family.'

2

Although both my parents were university teachers they were unable to enjoy the long vacation, as one could 'in the old days', according to my father, but were obliged to attend meetings, conduct interviews and carry out onerous administrative duties. So for a month every summer I was sent on my own to the country, holidays with my grandparents at the beginning and end of which Dad would deliver or collect me, staying a few days each time.

It was odd to arrive now in winter. We generally spent Christmas at home in Oxford, and made day trips to Mum's sister or her parents, Nana Sue and Táta Jiri, in Rickmansworth. The fact was that as a family unit we rarely saw my father's relations. This year, however, Grandpa had summoned his three children, asking them to make every effort to come, and to bring their families with them, for Christmas.

Now the bracken-covered lower slopes of the hill above the house were not a vibrant green but dull brown, as was the beech hedge on top of the brown stone wall that followed the curve of the drive. Plants overhanging the wall, cascading profusions of bright purple in summer, now had only dull green leaves. The trees that lined the drive or were dotted around the sloping fields were leafless, stark against the grey sky; Grandpa's wood beyond the lower fields looked glum, exhausted.

The drive led down from the road to the front of the house, whose imposing three-storeyed facade, with its eight sash-cord windows, each with four panes of glass but growing smaller as they ascended, always brought to my mind that great line from the Bible, 'In my Father's house are many mansions.' In summer each one of the eighteenth-century bricks from which it was built seemed to contain a range of sandy hues, but under this grey sky they presented a pale, bloodless uniformity. We drove on, past the wide and empty gravelled forecourt, following the drive as it continued, arcing around the garden and past the rather dilapidated coach house and outbuildings, to the parking bay by the stables. I was glad to see only one other car parked beside Grandma's butterscotch coloured Range Rover, Grandpa's saloon and Jockie's white Mini van: a bright, lime-green, brand-new Citroën Berlingo. One of those high square vans with the side panels replaced with glass and seats installed, for domestic use. Dad eased our muted, shapely veteran into the space beside it. 'I don't think we need to ask whose *that* is,' he said, chuckling.

'Pass me my dark glasses,' Mum said, joining in. 'What must it be like when the sun's out? Good Lord.'

The front door of the house opened, but no one emerged. Not a human being, at least. Instead, Grandpa's English setters shouldered their way out and came bounding across the yard. I got out of the car, bent down and opened my arms and they came straight for me, dark Leda almost knocking me over in her exuberance. Selena – Sel – the lighter one, hung back, trembling with excitement but shyer than her sister, until I called her in and she came. I buried my face in their hair, hugging them to me.

Sel reminded me of myself. A bewildering condition had over-taken me that previous spring. I'd always been one of the more confident children in my class at primary school. I was the first to put my hand up in answer to a question, or to volunteer for public speaking: I'd often read the prayers at assembly, and been the narrator of a dozen plays. While most children declaim their lines in a monotone aimed at the floor, teachers knew they could count on me to enunciate words clearly, lay stresses in the appropriate places, and project my voice to the audience. 'To paraphrase the great Zero Mostel,' Dad declared approvingly after one Christmas production of *Scrooge*, 'you reached the drunks at the back of the school hall, Theo.'

I continued in this manner during the first two years at comprehensive: talkative, ebullient, relaxed with girls as well as boys. Around Easter of this year, however, a sinister change had crept over me. I found myself weirdly uneager, unwilling, to speak in front of people other than my parents and my friends. Asked to read something aloud in class my eyes seemed to hesitate as they scanned the lines; letters blurred into one another. In conversation I'd think of something to say but then, instead of hearing it uttered, would become aware of the journey from my brain to my tongue, along which the words got jumbled up.

Sounds issued from my mouth that made no sense. I became, in short (though still in written tests that summer term one of the brighter kids in the year) an idiot. It's a characteristic of *Homo sapiens*, however, to adapt to changing circumstances and I soon developed a coping strategy: that of mentally rehearsing what I wanted to say before I said it. This involved visualising myself speaking, some moments in the future. The trouble was that by the time this rehearsal had taken place, as if in a small antechamber of my mind, conversation was liable to have moved on, so that even if I could say my piece without hindrance it rarely bore any relevance to what had since been said by someone else, and I looked an even bigger div than before.

This, I understood, was shyness, and its sudden onset inside me was a mystery, particularly since I'd always viewed other children who suffered from it with pity, if not contempt.

Matters were not helped by the fact that my voice was itself taking on a life of its own. Words burped from my lips, unpredictable eruptions. Deep growls, loud barks, high-pitched squeaks emerged, sometimes all within the same sentence. Other boys mimicked me, girls giggled behind their books, I was sure of it. I convinced myself that members of the public – in shops, on the pavement – would turn their heads upon overhearing me, startled, before turning politely away.

It was, fortunately, but a short step to the solution: silence. I stopped speaking. A remarkably successful tactic, it covered up my shyness, except when I blushed, which happened whenever someone expected me to talk. I turned what I knew to be an unlovely shade of puce, but remained defiantly mute: I didn't care what they thought. At least they wouldn't think I was a fool.

This secondary affliction, by the way, was one I'd inherited from my mother; the physical symptoms, at least, though in her case they had a different cause. Whenever Mum grew restless, irritated, building up to anger, blushing was the tell-tale sign. I was probably the only one who spotted it, though, because it was subtle, almost hidden. A gradual flushing of the skin of her neck, and then her ears becoming red (and both were often hidden, by collar or hair).

My companionable parents shared, on the surface, similar temperaments, but my mother was as passionate as my father was diffident, detached, amused by life. Her emotions were not, however, 'on show to the general public', as she put it. Public displays of emotion, in point of fact, were one of the many things that annoyed her – and brought that subtle blush to her neck. Others included battery farming, parking charges in hospital car parks, cosmetic surgery, fox-hunting, and all forms of injustice: she embarrassed me throughout my childhood by intervening in playground games if she thought a child was being bullied. Mum liked to engage me in argument on ethical issues from as far back as I could remember; she'd encourage me to form an opinion and then she'd disagree with it, not to indoctrinate me with her own views but for the pleasure of debate. And, I would come gradually to realise, to make me aware of the space we are all given in which to form our own moral ground, which she expected me to then defend.

I didn't reckon to suffer my shy affliction with Grandpa or Grandma – that summer's visit had been a lovely relief from it; with Jockie, the gardener, and Bronwen, their housekeeper, too, I'd been at ease. Maybe it was just because old people's hearing was useless: they didn't even seem to notice the fluctuations of my vocal cords. But the prospect of five days with my uncle and aunts and odd cousins – five days of nods, shrugs, shakes of the head in place of speech, of terse, mumbled replies, of stammering muteness – filled me, I confess, with dread.

3

The setters could not stay still, slobbering all over me, licking my face with their long wet tongues, enveloping me in their refulgent, meaty breath. Hugging Leda and Sel tightly to me, nuzzling my face in their thick winter coats, I experienced a great surge of happiness, followed by disappointment with the realisation that there were not only beautiful dumb animals but also human beings to be dealt with.

I opened my eyes, and stood up. While I'd been hiding behind the dogs, people had emerged from the house, and were exchanging kisses with my parents. Dad gave Auntie Gwen, his younger sister, a big, clumsy hug. Mum kissed Gwen's two daughters, my cousins. I could tell no one was sure whether to kiss each other's cheeks one or two or three times, but it afforded them all something to make an awkward joke about. Auntie Gwen gave me a hug, too. She was chunkier than my mother. She had a great mop of curly grey hair on her head, which frizzled my face as I leaned in to her.

'My, how you've shot up, Theo,' she said.

'Mum!' said Holly, the younger sister.

'I know, I know,' Gwen chuckled. 'Sorry, Theo, everyone must tell you that.'

We hadn't seen each other since the summer before last, but even before Gwen had spoken I'd noted that I was now closer in height to Dad than to any of the women standing in the yard.

The grown-ups exchanged their usual inanities – 'Good journey?' 'When did *you* get here?' 'Decent driving weather' – while my cousins and I stood in silence, until Holly said to me, while gesturing towards her mother, 'You going Afro too?'

I kind of shrugged and nodded at the same time. My tight curls must have twisted their way down my father's side of the family. Dad claimed to have had similar hair before he lost most of it, and had promised me he'd dig out a photo of himself from the nineteen seventies to prove it.

Sidney, who was fifteen, looked just like she had last time: thin as me (though more stick than wire, you might say), with flame-red hair and black-framed, over-sized spectacles just like her mum's, through which her large eyes peered at the world, seemingly confused by and at the same time somewhat delighted with it.

Holly, however, had changed. We were exactly the same age. Not quite the same birthday, but the same star sign. I should make clear that I did not believe in astrology; it was, in my opinion, absolute nonsense. 'Which is typical,' I'd told Holly, when we stayed with them on that weekend trip to their house in London eighteen months earlier, 'for a Scorpio,' which I thought was quite a good line. While Sid lay sunk in a beanbag, reading a book, Holly and I had spent most of our time in their garden together, playing badminton or bouncing up and down on their trampoline.

Now, standing by the cars, Holly appeared still tomboyish, in her stance and attire, but now her jeans were tight on curved hips, and layers of T-shirt and hoodie couldn't hide a definite feminine development in the upper regions. She was also now as tall as her elder sister. It was hard to believe they were siblings, red-headed Sid with her pale, angular features and smile that suggested she was trying to pay attention to you while not losing altogether some other thread of thought preoccupying her; while Holly was blond, with sallow skin, a pert nose, full lips and – possibly because of the brace she wore on her teeth – a strangely compressed smile that suggested some mischief had just occurred, or was about to. There was also something disconcerting about her gaze, and you only realised what it was if you studied her very closely: Holly was infinitesimally cross-eyed.

'Want a hand with your stuff?' Sid asked.

'We're sleeping all together in the nursery,' Holly grinned.

The boot of our car was full. I handed Sid and Holly Mum's laptop bag and walking boots, and my rucksack and guitar case. Then I noticed that my other cousin, Matt, had come out of the house and was saying hello to Mum. Shaking hands rather than embracing. If Holly had changed, her nineteen-year-old brother had undergone a weird transformation: my handsome cousin had cut short his long brown hair and dyed it the colour of strawberry roan; wearing a well-cut suit, it was apparent that he'd lost weight; the bone structure of his face had altered; and he was three or four inches shorter than he had been at the age of seventeen. Walking towards him, I understood that I was wrong, it wasn't Matt at all, but some other man. Moments later it became clear that this wasn't a man but a young woman – a school friend of Sid's, maybe? An orphan, perhaps? My brain underwent a dizzying series of reassessments while, laden with luggage, I trudged the short distance from the car across the patio. As I reached the stranger I saw that, up close, she was older than she had appeared from far away; much older, closer in age to Auntie Gwen than any of her children.

'This is my son, Theo,' Mum said. 'Theo, meet Melony.' What this woman's relation to anyone was, my mother – if she knew – didn't say. My hands were full, but I muttered hello on my way past, following Holly and Sid into the house.

Our footsteps rang on the flagstones in the open hall, the girls' voices echoed off the walls and up the wide staircase. Everything was as it had been when I was here in the summer except that the hallway was garlanded with Christmas cards: vertical displays stuck to strips of Sellotape hung from the ceiling, and pendant streamers of cards looped over lengths of string pinned to the corners of ceiling and walls. A backcloth erected for the performance for which we were gathering, as both performers and audience, of this family Christmas.

In the spacious drawing room, sofas and chairs had been shifted to make space for a wide, tall tree in the corner. Holly and I added a few wrapped presents to those already at its base. At its top a golden angel spread her wings an inch below the high ceiling. Strands of blue and silver tinsel, and fairy lights, were strung around the branches. The baby grand piano was in the opposite corner of the room.

'Where's Matt?' I asked.

'Coming straight from Uni,' Holly said. 'Still working on a production for his course. Get here later today.' She looked at her watch. 'At least, that's what he said.'

We walked through the room where the TV and Grandma's desk were – Sid had already returned to the sofa there, curled up with a book – and I found Grandma in the kitchen. She was sitting in her chair at the Aga. A pot of stew, or soup, simmered on the warm plate behind her.

'There you are, dear boy,' she said. 'I won't get up.' I bent down to hug her. We'd barely made contact before she barked in my ear, 'Yes, yes,' and fended me off, as if to say, All right, that's enough, we've got that formality out of the way. 'How are you?' she asked. 'Still growing? Good. Not smoking, are you?'

'Of course not, Grandma,' I said. I glanced at Holly and saw her smirking, and the combination of our complicity in the face of our grandmother's eccentricity and the way that Grandma said whatever she felt like, not giving a damn what anyone thought, had a naturally emboldening effect upon me, as it had in the summer. 'I'm only thirteen, Grandma.'

'Tommyrot,' she said. 'Your father was smoking on the sly at your age. I caught him behind the chicken shed.' Here she nodded in a vague direction outside. 'You know what I did with him?'

'No, Grandma,' I lied. 'No idea.'

'I made him smoke the rest of the packet, one fag after another.' She looked up at me and then at Holly with a smile of deep self-satisfaction. 'You never saw a child so ill. I left him throwing up in the grass and one thing I can assure you both: Rodney's not smoked another cigarette in his entire life.'

Apart from my Uncle Jonny and Aunt Lorna's mansion in north London – 'the monstrosity', as my parents referred to it – my grandparents' country house was the most impressive I knew. It had large rooms, spacious hallways and landings, with high ceilings and exposed wooden beams. It even had two staircases, so that if you wanted to avoid someone, or just needed a little privacy, the house obliged you.

The basement cellar had been converted by Grandpa into a study, and some store rooms, while the old nursery, at the top of the house, was where we children would sleep. As Holly helped me haul my stuff up the two flights of stairs, I calculated that ten adults and seven children could comfortably sleep in this building. Even without setting up extra camp beds or blow-up mattresses, which there was plenty of space to do.

'Yeah, it's a bit spooky,' she said.

In the nursery, which ran most of the length of the top floor, a series of alcoves had been cut into the eaves and a mattress placed in each one, creating half a dozen little billets. Holly and I dumped my stuff up there.

'That's mine,' Holly informed me, pointing to a rumpled duvet covered with clothes. 'Why don't you go next to it, and the twins can have the ones across from us?' She gestured towards my guitar. 'How much do they pay you?' she asked.

'Who?'

'Your parents.'

I looked at my cousin's face, but there was nothing there to help me work out what she might be on about. 'Pay me for playing my guitar?'

'Don't they pay you?' Holly shrugged. 'What's this big Christmas mystery, anyway?' Seeing my further incomprehension, she continued, 'Why we're here. Grandma and Grandpa asked everyone to come, right? Don't get me wrong, I mean, it's great, but why?'

'No idea,' I said, shaking my head. 'I guess we won't know till everyone's here.' Holly stared at me, as if she suspected I knew, but wasn't telling. 'We just have to be patient.' I looked away from her inquisitive gaze. There was a door at the end of the nursery. 'Have you been through there?'

'It's locked,' she said, making a face to show she'd tried it.

I walked past my cousin and, with the modest magnanimity of my greater knowledge of the house, reached up to the top of the door frame. I felt along it and soon discovered the key.

'I've never been in here,' Holly admitted as I unlocked the door, and entered. The room, illuminated weakly by the light from a single small window, was filled with old pieces of furniture and odds and ends. Wooden chairs, a towel rail, leather suitcases, a pair of roller skates, a tailor's dummy, a hatstand, framed paintings, a large porcelain bowl, a small chest of drawers, all covered with a coating of dust. It was like a forgotten junk shop, and was a striking contrast to the rest of the house, kept spotlessly clean by Bronwen, who came in four times a week and also laundered, ironed and helped Grandma with the cooking.

We poked around, until Holly started sneezing.

Downstairs, my father and the stranger, Melony, had joined Grandma in the kitchen. It was a long room, divided by a wide island, beyond which was the eating area: the dining table stood in front of a long set of sash windows that gave on to the great wide valley of the Corvedale, on whose far side lay Wenlock Edge. A soft drizzle was beading the glass.

'I love those berths where you lot are sleeping,' Melony told Holly.

'We did it when the first grandchild appeared,' Grandma told her. Not, 'We had it done,' or 'We paid builders to do it.' I imagined that Melony would assume our grandparents had done it themselves; would visualise them both up there, Grandpa sawing away, Grandma knocking in nails. It was her customary way of talking – 'We built the conservatory twenty years ago' – a kind of aristocratic boastfulness.

'The children seem to like it,' Grandma said with a shrug, as if this were no concern of hers. 'Can't imagine why they do, really. In the summer I let them stay in the summerhouse. Don't I, Theo?'

'I've seen foxes,' I told Melony. The effect Grandma had on my shyness seemed to be continuing. 'Seen a badger, tramping across the lawn in the moonlight.'

'I wish your grandfather would give you one of his guns,' Grandma said. 'Blasted things *destroy* my plants.' She looked to Melony with an expression that made the assumption of both understanding and support. 'The young today have no idea how to shoot,' she said, shaking her head in a long-suffering manner.

'I say, Ma,' my father interjected. 'I wouldn't have thought even you would be allowed to shoot protected species.'

Our attention was diverted by a strange squeaking sound from the TV area. Then Sid called out, 'Text from Matt. Message for you, Grandma.'

'Well,' Grandma demanded. 'What is it?'

'He'll be here in the morning.'

'Oh,' said our grandmother.

'He sends you hugs and kisses,' Sid called.

Grandma looked around at those of us assembled in her kitchen, nodding.

Our grandfather then appeared, up from his study downstairs. 'At last, my dear boy,' he said when he saw me. Grandpa and I hugged each other like we were two foreign presidents: with a certain ceremony, little more than chest to chest contact. He stood back and looked at me. 'I told your grandmother, after you left us in the summer, the next time we saw you you'd be taller than me.' He looked from Holly to me. 'Do you two youngsters want to get some air? Come and help me give the dogs a run.'

* * *

22

The drizzle eased as we climbed the drive and followed the lane along past the disused phone box, and turned off it up the track on to the hill. The dogs, who in the house lolled around as if drugged, came alive outside; they dashed about, noses to the ground, at great speed. They'd disappear from sight, then reappear in an unexpected place, full of mysterious purpose.

Once we reached level ground, and followed a path that skirted the hill on its western flank, Holly asked us to stop so she could take some photos of the view. 'I want to do a landscape painting while I'm here,' she said.

'Holly's an artist,' Grandpa informed me. 'She emails me her pictures sometimes. Don't you?'

This information, and what it suggested of Grandpa and Holly's relationship, surprised and, I admit, somewhat irked me.

'Drawings, mostly,' she said. 'They're rubbish, really.'

'Not at all,' our grandfather insisted. 'I think they're very fine.'

We walked on in the direction of Nordy Bank, and Grandpa told us stories of the English Civil War. 'This entire area, ripped apart,' he said. 'A mixed-up patchwork of loyalties to Parliament or Crown. But the folk I admire are those of Bishop's Castle and Clun, over there.' He gestured westward. 'Right by the border. They had a thousand men at arms but refused to fight for either side. They were prepared only to defend themselves from aggression.'

The soft rain resumed periodically. On our way back, still a mile or two short of the house, Grandpa paused, pointed to a tiny ruined cottage in the Corvedale below us – wet, grey stone and gaping slate – and said, 'That's where I was born, and spent the first years of my life.'

I stopped in my tracks, and saw Holly had done the same. She must have known, as I did, the story of our grandparents' extraordinary romance: how the clever local boy, orphaned, had been taken in by the lordly gentleman farmer – Grandma's father –and became inseparable from the farmer's daughter, and only child. They fell in love as children. Refused permission, at fourteen, to court her, Grandpa left without a word.

He returned for the first time ten years later, having established a market garden business little more than fifty miles – an hour or two's drive – away. Grandma's father, in the meantime, had come to the end of his savings, his energy, his resistance. Grandpa married Grandma and bought the house off his father-in-law. I'd never seen the actual place where Grandpa was born, had not considered his very earliest years. To peer now through the soft rain upon the mean hovel he came from, so close to the big house, was odd, another unsettling moment, as if (like his relationship with Holly) Grandpa had kept this sight hidden all my life and conjured it now with a cunning sleight of hand.

'I remember my early childhood more as I get older,' Grandpa said. Then he grimaced, and waved his hand, dismissing the personal. 'Everyone does. One's childhood becomes clearer. Rather like archaeologists revealing the distant past, or physicists working their way, as time goes on, further back, to the moment of the big bang. The moment before.' He gazed through the drizzle at the small grey cottage, beads of moisture in his white hair and moustache, the skin of his face damp. 'As if our memory is working its way back to the cosmic secret of our birth.' He looked at us and chuckled. 'You'll see what I mean one day.'

Back at the house, I took Holly to the stairs down to Grandpa's study and showed her the vertical display case of rocks he'd taken from the Shropshire Hills around us, during his recent geological explorations. At the bottom was the oldest, a lump of sedimentary rock found on the Long Mynd, from the Precambrian period. Above it was a piece of green sandstone from the Cambrian, found on Caer Caradoc, with the fossil of a delicate fern visible on its surface. On each shelf was a small sticker with the information.

'It's, like, a museum,' Holly said. I remembered with a stab of self-reproach for my idiocy that most teenagers view such places with disdain, as Holly surely would. 'Cool,' she whispered instead, and peered closer. Instantly it crossed my mind to invite her to Oxford and show her the Pitt-Rivers, which, as everyone knew, was the second greatest museum in the world.

On the next shelf up was a hard quartzite rock from the Stiperstones, dating back to the Ordovician period, named after a Celtic tribe, as was the Silurian period, represented by a piece of limestone taken from Clun Forest. Grandpa, I explained to my cousin, had unearthed these stones himself with his own geological hammer. I told Holly – as Grandpa had told me that summer – how the Church Stretton Fault ran through the Shropshire Hills, revealing strata of rock from different periods.

'It's a mecca for geologists,' I said.

'A mecca? What, like they go there to that hill and all walk seven times around it?' she said.

'That's good,' I said. I might have even chuckled a little. 'I like that. They go counter-clockwise.'

'With their sacrificial hammers.'

A lump of Old Red Sandstone, from the Devonian period, was dug from Grandpa's own property, while the black coal and the piece of dark basaltic lava were collected from the land above, upon which we'd just walked: the summit of Brown Clee Hill was still pockmarked with the ruins of abandoned buildings and quarries, from which basalt was taken to metal the roads of the Midlands. They were the youngest stones, but they were formed long before the Ice Age, in which glaciers covered most of the Shropshire hill country. It was only when the ice retreated that man had been able to move north and establish around here the first human settlements.

Holly got roped in to helping prepare something for supper, but I slipped out of the kitchen. I practised my guitar in the attic for a while, then I sneaked back downstairs, all the way to the basement. Rather like the locked room in the attic, Grandpa's study was unvisited by Bronwen, with her vacuum cleaner and duster: he wouldn't allow anyone to tidy up his den. Even in the mid-afternoon December gloom you could see what a mess the room was in, a clutter of books, maps, computer printouts, handwritten notes scattered across every surface. As I entered, Sel's black tail beat on the carpet. The study had three walls covered in books, and one wall of glass looking out to the lawn. There was a pool of light on the desk, where books and papers were laid out. Grandpa sat motionless, upright in his chair. I walked around the front of the desk: my grandfather was asleep, breathing quietly. When he exhaled, the white hairs of his moustache quivered. His mottled hands were folded on his stomach. I tiptoed back out of the room.

4

The rain had once more eased. Two ropes hung from a branch of the sycamore tree on the bank between the stables and the outbuildings. One had a car tyre tied to its end, the other a stick you could sit or stand on. Holly grabbed hold of the tyre and I the stick, and we climbed the bank as far as we could before, on the count of three, launching ourselves into gaping space and, by the end of the arc, a vertiginous height. It made your stomach lurch every time. As she swung, Holly shrieked. Myself, I managed to quell the same urge and maintain a manly silence.

Gradually, your body became accustomed to this gravitational surprise; the panicky swoon in your belly subsided. Swinging out, you looked down at the ground far below with indifference. Holly stopped screaming. The atmosphere was very still. Jockie was intermittently visible amongst shrubs in the garden below us; occasionally he took a forkful of stuff over to a bonfire, from which a weak pall of smoke rose. Otherwise the scene was deserted. Grandma had lied on the phone to me, or had perhaps forgotten: she *had* got rid of all the horses. On my summer visits there were always people around the stables: local kids whom Grandma let ride the ponies, and were mucking out or saddling up or hosing down the concrete yard. Now the stables, and the fields, were empty.

Holly and I were probably both becoming bored – and one of us might have had the gumption to say so before too long –

when the third and final family arrived. A large grey tank-like vehicle with tinted windows and a blunt nose like that of a giant pug dog cruised along the drive below and up past us and around to the parking area. Set high off the ground, it looked like a bullet-proof, militarised people carrier. The front door opened and Dad and Auntie Gwen's brother, Uncle Jonny, climbed down from the driver's seat. He stood, hands on hips and legs astride, gazing towards the outbuildings and shaking his head – ignoring Holly and I, who were surely within his peripheral vision.

In a voice that rumbled out of his barrel chest and across the yard, Jonny said, 'I *can* not believe it.' He wore nothing warmer than blue jeans and a white shirt, its top two buttons undone, dark chest hair sprouting from the gap. He gave the impression he didn't feel the cold. His siblings had emerged from the house and were trotting cheerfully towards him. By this time Aunt Lorna had got out from the passenger side of the car, and so had the twins, one after the other.

'I can *not* believe this,' Jonny growled, emphasising the third syllable through gritted teeth.

'What's up?' Dad asked as he reached his brother. They each turned to face each other and hugged, then Gwen did, too, before she moved on to Lorna, who was coming around the front of the vehicle. Holly jumped off the tyre and I followed her over.

Uncle Jonny pointed to the far end of the coach house. 'Pa promised me,' he said. 'Gave me his solemn bloody *word* he was going to find someone to get rid of all that crap.'

We all gazed across the yard. What Uncle Jonny was indicating with his accusatory finger was a collection of remains of old farm machinery. Relics of generations of scratchers of the land: ploughs, wagons, tractors, carts. Rusting sheets of metal and odd shapes of iron; rotting sections of wood. This pile, this quietly disintegrating museum, this clutter, must have been there all my life. I'd never really noticed it before. Now that it had been pointed out by my uncle, however, I felt a tingle of indignation, if only on his clearly aggrieved behalf.

'How's anyone ever going to be able to develop anything around here with that mess there?' he said, but then abruptly shifted focus. Before Dad could say anything, Uncle Jonny exclaimed, 'Holly! Not seen you for *months*. Theo! Good God boy, you're as tall as your father. Give me a hug.'

I felt myself enveloped in Uncle Jonny's bear-like, after-shave-musky embrace. 'And just as weedy as he was, too. Another skinny ribs. Amy!' he yelled at Mum, who was coming out of the house with Melony. 'There's no meat on this boy!' He let loose his embrace, but gripped my right shoulder with his left hand and grasped my left cheek with the fingers of his right hand. Actually, I was wrong: my uncle wore his shirt with the top *three* buttons undone – four if you count the one on the collar. 'We'll fatten you up, boy, don't you worry.' He let go of my cheek then patted it, before turning towards the others.

My uncle was utterly unlike his brother. I felt sorry for being so bony. We'd recently been given leaflets, and a cautionary talk, at school about obesity, which had made me wonder why it was that most academics, to whom the idea of exercise never seemed to cross their preoccupied minds, were thin as pencils. Apart from the obvious fact that most of them walked and cycled around Oxford, as my parents did, I'd come to the conclusion that they would have stuffed their greedy faces between meals like normal adults, but simply forgot to do so.

* * *

Aunt Lorna had jet-black hair, black eyes, brown skin. She was, Holly whispered in my ear, one of the most glamorous women in London. When she kissed me she stroked my cheek with her right hand, as if reluctant to let go of this agreeable moment of intimacy. 'So wonderful to see you, Theo darling,' she confided, in her voice with its trace of a foreign accent, a trace that mingled in my mind with the delicate scent of her perfume.

The grown-ups, laden with luggage, moved towards the house, leaving Holly and myself facing the twins. Since the last time I'd seen them I'd forgotten, I now realised, how to tell them apart. There was a definite if tiny physical distinction between them, a series, in fact, such that could be circled in a Spot-the-Difference double portrait, but I couldn't remember for the moment, scanning their cherubic, corpulent faces – cloned mini-versions of their bullish father, prettified by their mother's genes – what these were.

The twins were a year younger than Holly and myself, and I wondered whether they would remain identical through the fermentation of their own imminent adolescence. Would their voices break in unison, acne erupt in the same places; would they wake at night from the same sticky dreams?

'Come and see the car,' one of them said, climbing back into their vehicle.

'You already showed me,' said Holly.

'That was ages ago,' he replied.

'You haven't seen this one,' said the other. 'We only had it delivered last month.'

I gathered that the two London families, who lived on opposite sides of the capital, saw barely any more of each other than they did of their Oxford relations. Between us we comprised a triangulation of families whose sibling parents had, I supposed, little in common beyond having grown up together, so that I'm not sure it occurred to them how much we cousins, their children, might enjoy spending time together. Once everyone was inside the vehicle one of the twins slid the door shut, and we squeezed on to the back seat. There was a large space in front of us, like in a London cab, only bigger.

'We removed a row of seats this morning,' one of the twins explained.

'Look behind you,' said the other. 'Two more seats swing down from the sides when we need them.'

I wondered why this family of four travelled around in such a comically exaggerated vehicle. It was as if the parents would have preferred to have twice as many children as they did and in some way imagined that if they bought a spacious automobile it would suddenly, magically, fill with extra children. Which in a sense it did. The twins informed us that their people carrier was necessary to transport their friends with them to archery class, bridge club, Mandarin lessons, etc., etc. I knew at once that they were skitting us, that neither of the twins had friends of their own, such was the exclusive nature of their relationship.

'We had extra large screens installed,' said one, pointing a remote at the roof, from which two flat-panel monitors, each larger than our TV at home, opened out of an overhead pod. 'You can adjust the angle,' he said, making them swivel.

'Slot-loaded DVDs,' said the other. 'Integrated for CDs and MP3s too.'

'High brightness screens,' said the first. 'LCD.'

'Naturally,' his brother agreed. 'I mean, it's theatre-quality performance.'

'A cinema experience inside your car.'

'You ought to get one,' the first twin said, looking straight at me with a blank expression, so that it was impossible to tell whether or not he was being serious. It was an attractive prospect – perhaps watching telly in the car, unlike reading, wouldn't make me sick – but I wasn't sure what Dad would think about all this stuff clamped inside the chassis of his beloved Morris Traveller.

'We can watch the same film,' said one twin, 'or different. We have our own headphones.'

'Artiva T5s,' said the other, holding his set up. 'Wireless.'

'Obviously,' his brother added.

I'd been staring at my cousins as much as was politely possible, but I still couldn't spot any of their distinguishing marks. Finally, I ran out of patience and asked them straight out, 'Which one of you is which?'

'It's simple,' said one.

'Straightforward,' his brother agreed.

'Xan has a fleck of green in the pupil of his left eye.'

'Baz's ears are larger than mine.'

'Xan's ears are too small, in other words.'

'My eyes are closer together, too.'

'He's got a mole on his neck, just there, see?'

'And Baz has an extra freckle or two on his forehead.'

Holly was nodding. 'That's right,' she said, and the thing was that once you'd identified each of these miniscule features – Xan and Baz facing helpfully towards me, so that with quick glances I could compare one with the other – it was indeed easy to distinguish between them.

We climbed down from the car and the twins began walking towards the house. 'Don't you want a hand with your stuff?' I asked.

Neither stopped walking, but Xan threw over his shoulder, 'Oh, someone else will do that.'

'Hello?' Holly mimed a theatrical flourish of her arms to either side and raised her shoulders, a gesture rather wasted on her cousins, who had their backs to us. 'Like, *who*, for instance?' she demanded, and I recalled that Uncle Jonny and Aunt Lorna had all sorts of either daily or live-in help (or 'servants', as Mum referred to them) in their north London home.

The twins stopped at this point, and turned around. Baz marched towards Holly and I, and shouldered his way between us. We turned, to see Jockie pushing a wheelbarrow full of gardening tools into the storeroom at the end of the stables.

'Here, Jockie,' Baz called towards him. 'Would you mind very much sticking our bags in the conservatory?'

Jockie rested the barrow on its back legs and scuttled across the yard in quick, rheumatic little steps. He wore a dark three-piece suit, which only when he came close could you see was stained and frayed. He was, as everyone knew, precisely the same age as Grandma – seventy-five – and his father had worked here for Grandma's father, and they'd been exactly the same age, too.

Jockie began unloading items from the boot of the giant car.

'Are you sure you wouldn't like them taken right inside?' he asked. 'Into the entrance hall?' Standing beside Baz, Jockie, you could see, wasn't much taller than the twins.

'No, the conservatory will be fine, Jockie,' Xan told him expansively. 'We'll take it from there.' He and Baz strode towards the house. Holly was still standing there with the same expression of outraged puzzlement. I wondered what Mum would say to me later were she watching this scene out of one of the windows.

'Let me take the big one,' I said, reaching to lift a leather suitcase, which Jockie was attempting to drag over the lip of the car boot. He leaned neatly across, managing to block my way.

'I've got 'em,' he said. 'No problem for Jock. You get on in, Theo.' Using his shoulder, he eased me with surprising force out of the way.

Holly and I traipsed across the patio. Dusk was falling.

5

My parents had been given – or perhaps had asked for, I wasn't sure – the 'blue' bedroom, at the top of the stairs. Aunt Gwen was in the 'yellow' room at the end of the corridor, Jonny and Lorna in the 'red' bedroom to the left of the stairs – designations which bore no relation to actual colours, on the walls or anything else. These terms referred to some earlier era of decorative scheme, one assumed, and despite subsequent refurbishment were kept in current, confusing use.

Across the landing from Mum and Dad was my grandparents' wing, which consisted of their large bedroom and en-suite bathroom, and also Grandpa's dressing-room, which had a small divan bed in it where when I was younger I was allowed to sleep when I stayed in the summer. I would lie there in the mornings while Grandpa shaved at the small sink. He had an ancient radio on the shelf permanently tuned to Radio 4, and would talk back to the people on the *Today* programme as if it were being broadcast personally to him; would admonish the presenters when he thought they were rude, say 'Humbug!' to guests, groan at the latest Test score. He called everyone by their Christian name, thanking Charlotte for reading the news and Gary for the sport. It was a peculiar thing to do. I've been disconcerted recently to catch myself doing the same.

Where Melony was going to sleep I didn't know. There was a narrow landing up on the top floor, before you went into the converted attic space with its sleeping berths in the eaves. I'd noticed a bag and a pile of books on the bed there and assumed Sid had nabbed it.

My father was reading the newspaper on one bed. I lay on the other, watching Mum put make-up on at a table with a tilting mirror. I told my parents that we had a project next term in Sociology on 'Regions of Britain'. I had the idea to prepare a talk on regional accents, using recorded examples of my own family. Grandpa had an old tape recorder I could bring into service; otherwise I might be able to borrow the dictaphone which Baz had mentioned Uncle Jonny carried with him everywhere.

In the three and a half hours since our arrival, I told my parents, I'd noticed all sorts of subtle differences between us. Grandma spoke like the Queen, I explained, and Uncle Jonny did the same, as did the twins. Aunt Lorna's accent was similar except that she was clearly foreign, and as we were an island nation of immigrants it was just as well to have a recent example. Grandpa, on the other hand, had a less posh, more neutral accent than Grandma, and his was the one the elder son, my father, had copied.

'Steady on,' Dad said.

'That's not a criticism,' I reassured him. 'Because I've copied it too, from you.'

'With the occasional Cherwell gangsta lingo added,' Dad said.

Mum, I continued, had a similar accent to her son and husband, but whereas certain words pronounced by Dad betrayed his upper-class origins ('hise' for house, for example) and his slide down the social ladder, so different words spoken by Mum (like 'sile' for sale) indicated the Greater London suburbs she came from and her own climb up a similar number of rungs, to where they'd met.

At this point my father said I sounded uncharacteristically, and unpleasantly, precocious. He also mentioned that certain birds, such as chaffinches, had regional accents.

My mother objected that what I was talking about was much less to do with region than with class. 'I haven't finished,' I said. My throat ached, and I realised that I'd not spoken so much in ages. I described the way that Auntie Gwen – who worked for the Borough of Lambeth or the council of Brixton or something – only sounded so different from the rest of her birth family if you failed to listen carefully. In fact, her accent was similar to Dad's (and her vocabulary, too) but what she did in order to disguise her well-to-do upbringing was to swallow every syllable. Which, in turn, made you realise that what Grandma and Jonny and the twins did was to drawl all the time.

'Sid and Holly are different again,' I said in conclusion, 'from each other as well as their mother. Sid talks more like Dad and me, which may be a result of reading books, while Holly talks more like a proper cockney. Or at least what people call a Sarf Londoner.'

'Very observant, Theo,' Dad said. 'We'll make an anthropologist of you yet.'

'I still think it's more about class,' Mum insisted. 'Which is no less interesting. See what Mr Tiler says.'

It was quite impressive the way Mum remembered the names of all my teachers, even at secondary school. I'm not sure my father could have named a single one of them. 'I could record Jockie, too,' I suggested. Despite his name, Jockie had famously never been within two hundred miles of the Scottish border, but was a true Salopian, born and bred in the Corvedale. 'And as for

Bronwen,' I added, 'you couldn't get any more regional than her. I bet she still speaks Welsh.'

On top of the mahogany chest of drawers was a framed photograph of my father, aged fifteen or sixteen, riding a pony rounding up sheep on one of the hills around here. I realised that, of course, he and my aunt and uncle were back in the same rooms they'd grown up in. A single Airfix model of a camouflage-coloured Spitfire hung by a cotton thread from a tack embedded in the ceiling, and on the windowsill stood a row of hand-painted medieval knights, traces of Dad's childhood remaining from the successive clearances and refurbishments since his departure.

'It's serious, then?' Mum said, staring at herself in the mirror as she applied mascara to her eyelashes. My mother rarely wore make-up; when she did, it looked as if she were putting on some slightly weird fancy dress.

My father murmured agreement as he turned a page of the newspaper.

'You think so?' Mum asked.

'Sure,' he said.

Mum made eyes at herself and, satisfied with her work, pushed back the stool and stood up. 'Brave to bring her here, though,' she said. She started to unwrap the large blue towel around her. My parents had always wandered around our house in whatever state of undress they felt like, and indeed still did, despite my registering numerous official complaints.

'Wait,' I cried, swinging my legs off the bed. 'It's all right, I'm leaving.' The last thing I needed to see was my mother's naked bits and pieces.

* * *

Auntie Gwen and Melony were helping Grandma in the kitchen. My grandmother spotted me before I could slip past and ordered me to finish laying the table. I put glasses out, and then reached up to get the water jug shaped like a fish, and filled each glass. The water made a hollow glogging sound as it gulped out of the spout.

As I walked through my grandparents' sitting area, Grandpa was showing the twins his barograph, with its infinitesimally slowly revolving cylindrical drum, driven by clockwork. A sheet of paper was wound around it, on which an ink pen marked the atmospheric pressure, giving an indication of change in the weather. When I stayed in the summer Grandpa let me help him change the paper – spares were kept in a tray at the base of its oak case – and refill the ink knib. We'd polish the bevelled glass together.

'An aneroid barometer,' Grandpa explained to the twins. 'It measures small changes in air pressure, using a metal alloy that expands and contracts.'

'But I can get the weather in two seconds,' Xan objected.

'On his PDA,' Baz confirmed, pulling his own from his pocket as Xan did likewise, whereupon they competed to see who could summon up a forecast the quickest.

'What's your postcode?' Xan asked Grandpa.

Sidney was slumped in a chair. I bent down to see the cover of the book she was reading. Becoming aware of my presence, Sid peered up at me, eyes blank behind her glasses. Then she closed her book, the forefinger of her left hand inserted to keep the place, and with her right hand felt above her head: isolating a single red hair, she tugged it from her scalp and placed it in the book where her finger had been, before putting the book on the table beside the chair and following me through to the drawing room.

Dad and Uncle Jonny were sitting either side of the fire. Holly was perched on the arm of Jonny's chair, but when she saw us she came over, and the two sisters asked each other what was being rustled up in the kitchen, and how long it was going to be. Holly wore a tight T-shirt and a short skirt over tights with multi-coloured, horizontal stripes. The colours of the rainbow were in them, probably; circling, one above the other.

'Theo's staring at Holly's legs,' Xan announced loudly. I'd not been aware of the twins coming into the room behind me. Sid and Holly turned their attention towards me.

'No, I'm not,' I stuttered.

'He's blushing,' said Baz.

'Too close to the fire,' I mumbled, edging even further away from it than I already was, and from my cousins.

'The tights look cool, don't they?' Sid said. 'I got them to put in her stocking, but she didn't want to wait.'

'Not after our parents agreed we wouldn't do stockings this year,' Holly said.

'Be careful what you say,' Baz admonished her. 'My brother still believes in Santa Claus.'

'So does Baz, actually,' said Xan.

'Exactly,' Baz agreed.

Mum was sitting on one of the sofas, talking with Aunt Lorna. Both of them had dressed up for dinner, in their own ways. My mother had little interest in clothes. She objected to shopping on principle, an imposition upon her time. All her and Dad's clothes came from Marks & Spencer online – her idea of a shopping spree was the acquisition of a brand-new pair of walking boots from Milletts – and she was glad that nowadays I was happy to mooch around town buying my own.

Aunt Lorna, on the other hand, could have been the very model for the clothes she wore. She never grew older, for one thing. Seeing my poor mother next to Lorna made me wonder whether it was the admin, the research – shut up in her study or at a desk in the Bodleian Library – or the actual teaching that had aged her. Probably all three.

Aunt Lorna worked as an interior designer, which, according to my father, was someone who was paid by a client to tell them what colour paint to put on their walls and where to put their furniture, although Lorna didn't actually do that work herself, she only advised. Uncle Jonny earned so much money that she didn't need to do it; Lorna herself called it her hobby. 'I like to help friends,' she would say in her slightly foreign accent, and with a modest shrug.

Mum claimed that Lorna worked hard enough, running round the shops and on the treadmills in the gym, which she undoubtedly visited every day. But in actual fact my mother and my aunt had more in common than might have been expected: they were united in opposition to their mother-in-law.

My father, in Grandma's opinion, was a country boy who, after a youthful sojourn in the city, following his undergraduate studies with a doctorate, should by now have long since returned to the country. He could have taught in a local school or college, or even taken over Grandpa's business. It was Mum who kept us in Oxford, according to Grandma, she the Head of Department, competent and driven, quite at home in what Dad referred to as 'the trenches of academia'. He himself remained a junior member of staff who 'kept his head down', content to teach a little, do some research, publish the occasional article, fulfil the minimum of administrative obligations.

It was obviously true that, as Mum said, the decisions my parents made were 'none of her bloody business', but the thing was that I knew Grandma was right. When Dad had come to collect me from my month-long visit that August, and stayed for a long weekend, I'd gone to look for him one evening and found him in the field up above the house, sitting on the ground, leaning against the trunk of a beech tree. There was a glass of wine beside him, and he'd rolled himself one of his occasional cigarettes. I lay on the grass close by. It was only when he wiped his hand across his face that I realised my father had been weeping. After the moment it took me to recover from this unsettling sight, I asked him what he was sad about.

Dad shook his head. 'No, no, not sad, old chap,' he said, smiling. 'Not at all. I'm happy, very happy.' He opened his arms, gesturing forwards. 'Look.'

Gazing over the top of the house, I watched the sun setting beyond the Long Mynd across the valley, where a patchwork of green and brown fields was wreathed in a hazy, buttery light. Smoke rose from slow-burning fires, and drifted on the breeze. The Welsh hills around the western horizon were blue. You could see isolated homesteads; odd hamlets which, as Grandpa had told me, 'were already old when the Domesday Book was drawn up'.

Dad reached over and drew me to him. 'I just love it here, Theo, that's all,' he said. 'This landscape. To perceive it, to be in it, to become part of it. That gives me great happiness.'

Aunt Lorna's sin was even more specific. When Uncle Jonny had first brought her here, fifteen years earlier, she was enraptured by the house. 'Wow,' she said to Grandma, 'you could really do something with this place.'

Grandma was so insulted she'd refused to speak to Lorna for years. It had taken all Grandpa's powers of tact and persuasion to bring about a rapprochement when the twins were born, but even now Grandma rarely spoke to her daughter-in-law unless Lorna addressed her first. She had forgiven neither of them. 'You could really do something with this place,' however, had – unbeknownst to our grandmother – become a family catchphrase.

Grandma now came in to the drawing room. 'I've left Gwen in charge,' she said, a note of despair in her voice. 'I do hope she won't burn everything,' she added, as if this were a common occurrence whenever her daughter was let loose in the kitchen. 'Make way,' she said, shooing Dad out of her chair by the fire. 'Make way there.'

Dad went over to help Grandpa, who'd been waiting for Grandma's arrival, to pour drinks. My attention turned to the large portrait of my grandparents above the fireplace. Painted on the eve of their marriage, it displayed the young couple as owners of all they surveyed, of the landscape of their lives, of their destiny. One of Grandpa's dogs lay at his feet, the other stood a foot or two away. The portrait was commissioned by Grandma's father, his final grand gesture, after he'd sold the house to Grandpa, who'd done as he'd said he would: built a business up from nothing and come back for the hand of the woman he loved.

In the portrait Grandma sat side saddle on a fierce-eyed chestnut horse, which stood at a diagonal in the frame, facing the bottom right-hand corner of it. Grandpa stood in front of her billowing black skirt, his left arm resting across the neck of the horse, just in front of its saddle. They had been placed in a

43

formal pose, yet looked supremely relaxed, and assured. My father had told me that in his opinion it was a remarkable provincial painting. That the local artist had somehow suggested certain ambiguities in their relationship. Grandma did not wear a riding hat: her hair fell, a little loose, with the hint of a breeze. It was she who drew the spectator's attention. If this young woman wasn't exactly beautiful she was undoubtedly dramatic. Angular, graceful and powerful. You couldn't help thinking that she had tamed the horse, and the handsome man too. But then you looked at it a little longer and thought maybe he had tamed her. While in reality probably all three remained a little wild.

The contrast with how my grandparents looked now – each dressed similarly to the other, in plain sweater and trousers – made you realise how men and women become androgynous as they age: Grandma's strong features had sunk into her wrinkled face; her hair, grey and thin, was cut short. Grandpa put a glass of gin and tonic in her hand. They looked more like a pair of soft brothers now, or tough sisters, than the glamorous young husband and wife in the painting.

Uncle Jonny caught my eye. 'Over here,' he said, archly raising his eyebrows. I walked over, and waited, while he, too, waited, smiling slyly. 'Young man,' he said quietly, 'your father's told me how well you're doing at school, and I'd like to shake your hand.' We reached towards each other and shook hands with a certain mock solemnity. When I withdrew my hand, there in my palm, magically, was a note. The particular trick Uncle Jonny managed was to somehow make me press my own thumb against the note to keep it in place, and thus secret. In accordance with the spy-like element of the enterprise I unwrapped the note surreptitiously.

The note was slightly, strangely, larger than a normal one, and an odd salmon colour. For a moment I thought it was counterfeit. A joke. Then I saw that it was a £50 note. I felt light-headed. The thought that as soon as we got back to Oxford after Christmas I could buy the black-and-red Bentley bass guitar someone I knew had for sale, with its maplewood neck and rosewood fingerboard, and its own heavy padded black gig bag, made my heart glow with gratitude. 'Thank you, Uncle Jonny,' I said. He nodded, frowning, smiling in a seigneurial, Mafia-like manner. I tried to imagine Dad handing out money to his nieces and nephews like that. Quite apart from the absurdity of my skinflint father doling out fifty-pound notes, if he were to try it in that secret-agent way it wouldn't work: the note would come back, stuck to his own hand, or fall fluttering in full view to the floor. The idea almost made me laugh out loud.

We collected a warmed plate each, under Grandma's instruc-tion, and after Melony had served us with either couscous or rice, Auntie Gwen ladled roast vegetables: peppers and squash, garlic, parsnips, potatoes, carrots. They were delicious. There was honey roast ham for those who wanted it, purchased in Harrods' Food Hall that very morning by Uncle Jonny, and now carved by him. My mother, who was jointly responsible for her college wine cellar, 'and so knows a thing or two', Dad said proudly, had bought two boxes of wine as a contribution to proceedings, and was telling Grandpa about the vintage she'd chosen for this evening. Grandma decreed that those of us under sixteen should be allowed one glass each, diluted with water, 'in the French style', whether we wanted it or not.

Someone whose handwriting I didn't recognise had set folded tabs with our names on around the table, though I was quite sure it was Grandma's arrangement. She had her sons on either side of her, while Grandpa had Lorna to his right and Melony to his left. Xan sat between Melony and Mum, Baz between Mum and Auntie Gwen, who was next to Jonny.

I was in the middle on the other side, with Sid on my left, then Lorna, and Holly on my right between me and Dad. I could see that no one was sat next to someone from the same nuclear family, and was rather astonished that the twins had assented to this arrangement, which, I imagined, was not going to be much fun for Mum, stuck between them, since from the first mouthful Xan and Baz were leaning backwards to snigger to each other behind her back.

'Have you oiled the guns, Pa?' Uncle Jonny wondered in a loud voice, from one end of the table to the other, demanding that other, quieter conversations cease.

Grandpa turned to his left and explained to Melony – and reminded the rest of us – that he and Jonny had a tradition that they always went hunting together on Christmas Eve on a friend's estate. Melony asked what they shot, and Grandpa said they might bag a couple of rabbits, or a pheasant. Occasionally a deer. Surely, Melony questioned, you need to hang venison or game; you wouldn't eat it the day after it's killed.

'Oh no,' Grandpa said. 'You're absolutely right. This is for my son to take back to London. Share with his pals on New Year's Eve. Isn't that so?'

Dessert was a bowl of fruit served with a mixture of cream and yoghurt, with a layer of burnt sugar on top, one of Grandma's classic combinations, made by Bronwen before we'd arrived. Grandma was listening to Dad talking when suddenly she exclaimed, 'No. I'm sorry. I'm not having it,' with such vehemence that everyone turned towards her. 'Well?' she demanded, and ordered her son: 'Tell them what you just told me.'

My father explained that he'd recently given a talk, a guest lecture, to the Part-time Master of Arts course at the Department of Continuing Education 'down the hill', as he referred to the University of Oxford. (Mum, in turn, described Dad's place of work, Oxford Brookes University, as either 'the Poly' or 'up the hill', depending upon the state of her feelings towards him.)

The programme of this course consisted, apparently, of half a dozen four-day seminars and one week-long summer workshop. Chatting informally with the students afterwards Dad had been surprised to learn that one of them flew over from Vancouver.

'Seven long-haul return flights,' Grandma fumed. 'For a part-time course in . . .' She fluttered her hand at Dad in a way that suggested both her ignorance of his subject and its irrelevance. 'And the other one?'

'Another student,' Dad admitted, 'revealed that she was coming to Oxford from Los Angeles.'

'Do they not have universities in California any more?' Uncle Jonny asked. 'Has Arnie terminated all the centres of learning?'

But Grandma was in no mood to be deflected by flippancy. 'It's simply not good enough,' she said. 'No, I'm sorry, Rodney, it has to stop. I for*bid* you from teaching there again. Where are your principles? As for whatever paltry fee they pay you for doing this, it's nothing less than blood money.' Grandma's face was flushed, her voice was becoming as tremulous as it was strident. She seemed to be trembling with anger. 'As for you, Amy,' she said, turning to Mum, 'I would have thought that you might be in a position, and of a mind, to do something about it.'

Xan and Baz began simultaneously to snigger.

Grandma turned back to Dad. 'You can start by giving the money they paid you to those fine people trying to halt that *evil* expansion of Heathrow. In fact,' Grandma said, addressing the whole table once more, 'you should *all* join their campaign, if you've not signed up already. You younger ones especially. There's nothing I hate more than apathy amongst the young.'

There were nervous smiles, a tiny eruption of giggles from Holly, to join the twins' underhand titters. Our grandmother, furious now, stood up. Her chair fell backwards behind her. 'Do none of you understand the gravity of the situation?' she railed. 'This planet is choking. We, the human race, are killing this world. You are my children, my grandchildren, and you do nothing about it. *Nothing*.' She threw her napkin, which she'd picked off her lap as she stood up, back down on to the table. 'It's not good enough,' she decided. 'I'm not having it.' And she marched through the kitchen area and out of the room. We heard her steps angrily mounting the stairs.

If it hadn't been for Grandpa's presence, I suspect we would have all burst into embarrassed laughter. It was outrageous. What did Grandma know of what we were doing? Nothing? We were each one of us most likely doing plenty! Her accusations were unfair, her behaviour unhinged.

As it was, we stared at our bowls and took little sips of our drinks. The fact of the matter was our grandmother, we all surely understood, was going mad right in front of our eyes. Apart from the fact that when you thought about it you realised, after all, that she was right. Meanwhile, I stole a glance at my mother across the table, and felt immediately sorry for Dad, head bowed along the table from me, who, I knew, was really going to get it in the neck when they got back up to their room.

6

'Shall I give the dogs their biscuits?' I asked my grandfather. 'Thank you, Theo,' he said. 'And turn off the lights out there, would you?'

Grandpa had strung a cable from which hung different coloured light bulbs along the eaves of the stables and, from the corner nearest the house, overhead across the patio to the arched gateway down to the garden. Red, blue, green, yellow. I switched off the lights at the socket in the tack room and walked out beyond the yard, past the outbuildings. The dogs were sniffing around in the pitch-dark night. There were no stars visible above.

I thought back on Grandma's behaviour. It wasn't so much what she'd said, her accusations, her reference to my mother – a book could have been compiled of examples of her rudeness – as the fact that she had become so angry and upset: she was never usually affected herself by the way she treated others. She displayed only a haughty disdain. As for what she'd said, well, as I heard Mum whisper to Dad, 'They live all alone in this *mansion*, and lecture others on *energy* use?'

My parents and I rarely went abroad on holiday – preferring to stay in cottages on the British coast or go walking in the Welsh hills – and even then it was usually over the English channel by ferry. But they both flew off on occasions to deliver papers at academic conferences. The thing was that Grandma was right: it *was* up to us. I took a solemn oath on my grandmother's honour not to ever fly in an aeroplane again.

I whistled for the dogs and trotted back to the house. By the time I reached the back door they'd caught me up, and wriggled excitedly around my legs. I gave them each a Bonio from the tin on the shelf and patted them goodnight, before switching off the light and closing the door of the pantry.

Holly was still in the bathroom and the twins, one in each of the alcoves opposite ours, were explaining how the unfortunate – if unspecified – defects of Holly's personality were attributable to her parents' divorce, some years earlier. I couldn't remember my American uncle, Sid and Holly's father. Neither his name, nor his face. I could recall, faintly, the lilt of his Mississippi accent; his hair, grey and thinning, with a stringy little ponytail tucked, customarily, inside his collar; and his paunch. It was like how pregnant women looked beautiful for most of their term, their stomachs perfectly curved, but then – right at the end, as birth became imminent, I supposed – they became enormous, grotesque, with this great blob sticking out in front of them; like a space hopper was about to burst straight out of their navel. My uncle had a belly like a woman about to go into labour, which he bore proudly before him, but of his face I recollected not a single feature. He'd become in my memory like a character from a certain episode of *Doctor Who*: victim of an alien erasure, his face rendered blank.

'What many people don't realise, Theo,' Xan told me, 'is that divorce is like this massive electric shock. You see, every child imagines that their parents' relationship is secondary to – and somehow even a consequence of – the one he or she has with them.'

'I don't,' I objected.

'Ah, but you're an only child,' Baz pointed out.

'Exactly,' Xan agreed. 'The parents' relationship feels, to a *normal* kid, naturally, intuitively, subservient to the child's with them.'

'But divorce is a cruel rupture,' said Baz, 'which makes clear that the parents' relationship was always – and remains – *more* important.'

'Which comes as a terrible surprise,' Xan said.

'Which the child internalises into guilt, as being the one who *caused* the rupture.'

'I mean, you only have to look at Holly.'

'What about Sid?' I asked.

'Too old,' said Xan. 'According to Freud.'

'Quite,' said Baz.

I knew they were talking nonsense, but I wasn't sure how to prove it. My twin cousins went to a famous (or 'notorious', as my mother described it) private school, whose pupils sat their GCSEs as young as twelve; the most successful occasionally went up to Oxford or Cambridge at fifteen. Even the dayboys like Xan and Baz had to stay in school to do their homework until eight-thirty every evening, *and* go back in on Saturday mornings. Their half-terms consisted not of a week off, as comprehensive schools did, but one single Saturday morning. They had an *entire* free weekend. It almost made you feel sorry for them.

When Holly came up and climbed in to the pod next to mine Baz, opposite, informed her that on the third of September that year he'd been abducted by aliens.

'Oh yeah?' she said.

'Yes.'

'It's true,' said Xan. 'He was.'

'They conducted medical experiments on me.'

'Yeah, right.'

'She doesn't believe you,' Xan said.

'Fine with me,' said Baz. 'I'm not seeking publicity.'

'Show her the scars.'

'Actually,' Baz said, 'they detained me for fifty years.'

'Fifty years?' I repeated, idiotically.

'That's like about two minutes in earth time, Theo,' Baz explained.

'Seriously,' Xan said, nodding gravely. 'He did reappear after a couple of minutes. It's the truth. I was the only one who knew he'd gone. Go on, show them one of the scars.'

'Oh, all right,' Baz agreed. He climbed out from under his duvet. With a stoical reluctance he lifted up his pyjama top and pulled down the bottoms a little, revealing a neat scar in his lower abdomen.

'Right,' Holly said. 'That's not for an appendiceptomy, by any chance?'

Baz stared at her. 'She said a-ppen-di-cep-to-my.'

'Maybe she meant appendectomy,' said Xan, shrugging.

'I can't really show you the other scars,' Baz said. 'Seeing as you're a girl.'

'You could show Theo,' Xan suggested.

I wrinkled my nose, and declined the offer.

'You're grossing him out,' Xan said.

'At least he believes in the existence of non-terrestrial life forms,' Baz said, climbing back into his alcove. 'Unlike some people round here we won't mention.'

'Speaking of whom,' Xan took over, 'you've got to tell us, Hol.'

'I mean, you don't have to,' said Baz.

'But what's it like having a *les*bian for a mother?'

'He means having a mother who's turned *into* a lesbian.'

Holly shrugged. 'Some people think it's sketchy,' she said. 'But I think it's pretty cool.'

'You know her and Melony?' Baz asked. 'How do they, *you* know. I mean, when they do it. What do they do?'

'Ignore him,' Xan advised. 'Use YouTube like everyone else,' he told his brother.

'Melony's been trying to get pregnant,' Holly said, in a matter of fact way. She told us their plan was to mix Gwen's egg with the sperm of a gay friend of theirs, and when embryos began to develop they'd be put into Melony's womb. The twins and I listened in silence while Holly proceeded to tell us in unnecessary obstetric detail about intrauterine inseminations, cytoplasmic sperm injections, gamete fallopian transfers and other such outlandish fertility treatments.

'They sound almost as disgusting as the natural method,' said Baz.

'How do you know all this stuff?' Xan asked.

'They talk about it all the time,' Holly said. 'It hasn't worked yet, but they're still trying.'

'When our mother was pregnant with us,' said Xan, 'she told us she had, what was it?'

'Wrestler's legs,' his brother declared.

'Precisely. Wrestler's leg syndrome. She's all right now, you'll be glad to know.'

'She's still a very good runner, actually,' said Baz.

I told them about this Australian frog I'd read about in Biology, which swallows its eggs: they hatch in the stomach and the tadpoles swim around in the inky blackness until they become frogs, when they pop out of their mother's mouth.

'Up to twenty-five of them,' I said. 'Like coins from a fruit machine.'

At that moment, as if in response to my snippet of natural history, Holly broke wind, with a loud, wet, bubbly and protracted noise.

'Holly!' said Baz.

'That wasn't me,' she protested. Baz and Xan sniggered in their alcoves. 'What's going on?' She farted again a moment later, and this time it was Xan who berated her. The third time, Holly jumped up as if she'd been bitten, bashing her head against the roof of her pod, which seemed abruptly to make her fart again. I realised that the twins had planted something in her alcove. It was a pathetically puerile kind of humour, and I thought I was going to be sick with suppressed laughter. I had to hide my face in my sleeping bag and bite the fabric. Holly climbed out and pulled everything after her – pillow, duvet, sheets, mattress – until she found the speaker the twins had placed there, and which one of them was operating with a remote control.

I wasn't sure what time things eventually quietened down. Not before a false lull, during which it appeared that I was the one to start blowing off: the other twin had planted a speaker under *my* mattress. This repetition was almost as funny as the first one. Holly at least seemed to think so. She claimed that men pass wind between fifteen and twenty-five times a day, according to official National Health Service figures; while women only fart ten times, 'and a lot more quietly'. Xan told her she wasn't so screwed up after all, that Sidney was the screwball in her family, at which Sid's voice carried through from the landing: 'I can *hear* you.'

None of us mentioned our grandmother. Instead we turned off the lights and in the dark fell into an argument about the ethics of carrying knives.

'I mean,' said Xan, 'I'm not saying it should be obligatory.'

'If you don't want to,' Baz agreed, 'you shouldn't have to.'

'But every citizen has a duty to defend himself,' Xan opined.

'Only cowards carry weapons,' said Holly.

'And idiots,' I said.

'Well,' said Xan, 'obviously no one in Oxford needs to carry a shank.'

'Unlike the ghetto of Hampstead Garden Suburb,' said Holly.

When we'd run out of words, there were fake snores in the silence, which were almost as funny as the farts. It was a raucous night.

As things finally settled, I reflected upon the fact that, back in Oxford, I rarely noticed how quiet our house was. Occasionally, however, a friend would come round after school. At first, they wouldn't notice it either. If one or other of my parents were at home, which was unlikely (I'd had my own front door key for as long as I could remember) they'd do little more than return my greeting from their desk. My parents, as I've already intimated, were content to live in companionable tranquility, threaded with the rippling stream of their conversation or by Beethoven piano sonatas on our stereo. It was left to me to provide a snack for my guest and take him to my room, where I'd show him the chessboard or the Lego or my collection – like my father before me – of hand-painted knights of medieval Europe.

It was only gradually, as we played in the silence of my bedroom, surrounded by the greater silence of the house, that my companion's face would begin to betray his unease, and puzzlement – which I think was actually more intuitive than conscious. He would stop what he was doing, sit motionless, ears cocked. He would look towards the door, then, after some moments, shrug to himself, and resume whatever activity we'd been amusing ourselves with. Once I was playing backgammon with a boy called Billy Lake when he frowned, gazed at the walls of the room, and said, 'It's like a tomb in here, isn't it?'

Or, sometimes, I'd go to a friend's house, and the opposite experience occurred – although, in truth, I noticed the difference immediately: other people's parents yelled at them, siblings squabbled, snatched things from each other, played awful music on their docking stations. And the games we played were on PlayStations, PSPs, Nintendos, the machines bleeping and squawking like hysterical birds. Televisions were switched on and left on, volume set high, even when no one was watching any more. Overexcited dogs yapped. Conversation was conducted in loud, disputatious tones.

My cousins were used to the jostle, the cut and thrust, of family life. I resolved to participate. Back in our grandparents' house, surrounded by relatives, my shyness seemed to have had its strangulating hold weakened. This week, it seemed to me, had every possibility of being the best Christmas of my life.

II

I

I was useless at sleeping late in the mornings. 'You'll improve,' my father claimed; but he'd been saying so for years. I'd always been the first to wake in our house, and would enact protracted battles with my knights and cowboys or drag my duvet to the sofa downstairs and watch TV until one or other of my parents emerged.

So it was in the attic of my grandparents' house. I awoke in my alcove as if in a space shuttle. My cousins in their own pods looked as if they might sleep for a few more light years yet, so I pulled on some clothes and trod silently downstairs. My grandparents, fortunately, were early risers like myself. My grandmother was sitting beside the Aga in her thick blue dressing gown, a mug of tea warming her hands. Grandpa was outside the window that looked out from the kitchen sink, replenishing with nuts and seeds the bird feeders which he'd strung along a washing line. Beyond him, Jockie was at work already. He'd had a hair cut overnight, short as a soldier. And it must have been mild out there, because he was wearing shorts. His legs, I remembered from the summer, were woody, their skin like bark. The old gardener looked boyish.

'Jockie's here on Christmas Eve,' I observed.

'He would in*sist* on coming,' Grandma said with a long-suffering air. 'I suppose I'll have to find him something to do. Did you hear the telephone ring in the early hours?'

I told her that I hadn't.

'Matt,' she said. 'Left me a message on the answerphone. He's not sure he can get here today, it'll probably be tomorrow, but even so he's going to make *every* effort.'

'That's good,' I said.

'Poor boy,' Grandma said. 'Organising the *entire* production with no help whatsoever. Make yourself a cup of tea, Theo. You know where things are. I'm glad you're up. I want to ask you something.'

Rather than wait until I'd made my own weak mug of sweet tea and could give her my full attention, Grandma addressed me as I moved around the kitchen.

'My car,' she said. 'I don't want it any more, you see?'

I had the idea that Grandma's butterscotch Range Rover was older than I was. Certainly I could not remember a time when she drove a different vehicle.

'Don't you need it?' I wondered.

'I don't *wish* to need it,' she said.

Everyone knew how much Grandma loved her Range Rover. She drove that majestic vehicle around the Shropshire Hills, sovereign of her domain, to point-to-point meetings, animal breeders, remote plant nurseries. Often there'd be a trailer attached, with a pony inside. That last summer I'd gone with her to Presteigne as she delivered a rescue pony she'd nurtured back to health to the grateful granddaughter of friends of hers. Another day we collected a problematic gelding she'd agreed to stable while she diagnosed its psychological shortcomings. She was known, it seemed to me, to everyone. 'How are you, Mrs Cannon?' they'd ask. 'Fine, thank you,' she'd reply – without ever mentioning *their* name, I noticed. 'Now, where is this troublesome beast?'

'I simply don't have the time or the patience, Theo,' she'd

confided in me, 'to remember everyone's name around here. But don't worry, I know whose family everyone belongs to.'

She liked to pay occasional weekend visits to us in Oxford, or the others in London, pretty much unannounced. 'I'm on my way,' she'd declare on her mobile, somewhere on the M40, and soon that distinctive, mud-splattered vehicle of hers would cruise into the city, and park outside our house. Grandma always brought a box of home-made jams, pickles, bottled fruit; eggs, mushrooms picked by Grandpa out walking the dogs on the hill that very morning. 'Gifts from the country,' she'd say, handing the box to her daughter-in-law, as if we were the victims of urban deprivation, she the generous representative of rural plenty.

My grandmother never stayed the night. She'd join us for lunch then turn back for home. 'Better get back before dark,' she'd say. 'Need to shut the hen house.' Or, 'You know how much I hate driving at night. Modern headlights dazzle me.' If the weather was dreadful Dad would beg her to stay, but she never did; would head for home through torrential rain, back to her own bed; her mug of tea beside the Aga in the morning; the house she'd lived in all her life.

'No married couple requires two cars,' she told me now. 'Certainly not old fogies like us. Your grandfather or Jockie can ferry me around. I know your uncle probably has three or four vehicles,' she said, holding her hand, palm out, towards me, as if I were about to bring up Uncle Jonny myself. 'I'm not interested. I'm talking about the lead one takes around here, and having two cars gives *quite* the wrong message.' She cleared her throat, and said, 'Do you want it?'

I gulped a mouthful of hot tea, which I had then to swallow, scalding my mouth and throat.

'I've offered it to the girls,' Grandma said. 'They've declined. Good for them. How about you?'

Was this a riddle? I had no idea whether my grandmother wanted me to say yes or no. 'I'm only thirteen,' I said. 'I can't drive.'

'Really?' she said, genuinely surprised. 'By the time he was your age your father could handle pretty much any motor vehicle you gave him. Learned to drive in Jockie's Mini van, up and down the drive, endlessly.'

We drank our tea in silence for a while.

'I'm *certainly* not giving it to the twins,' Grandma said, for reasons apparently too obvious to require spelling out. She raised her eyebrows at me, in such a way as to suggest we'd been competing to crack a code, and she got it before me. 'I suppose I could give it to the chickens,' she said.

The dogs were sniffing around the coach house. I found Grandpa loading logs into a wheelbarrow, and I volunteered to take them round the side of the house and in through the French windows of the drawing room, to stack in the box to the side of the fireplace. I returned the barrow to the coach house, and loaded it up with more logs, ready for the next day. When I looked outside, I saw that someone else was up: dressed in black running tights and top, black gloves, trainers, Aunt Lorna was performing warm-up exercises, using as apparatus the wooden picnic table on the patio. She placed her left heel on one of the benches, and with both hands on her left thigh, just above the knee, and her spine straight, she tilted her torso towards her left leg. Lorna stayed in this position for some seconds, then relaxed, stood up, and did the same with her right leg.

Aunt Lorna was stretching the muscles beneath her skin. She was also demonstrating, to anyone who happened to be watching – to her thirteen-year-old nephew – in what precise way a woman's body was beautiful: like this, placing her left foot now up on the table, putting her hands on her left knee and leaning the weight of her body forward. The muscles of her curved buttock stretching. Like this. Lorna swapped legs. Relaxing, she gazed around. Her eyes rested, for a moment, on mine. I didn't think she could see me, in the coach house, but I took a step or two backwards just in case, deeper into the shadows.

Now, feet back on the ground, Lorna lunged forwards onto her left leg, knee bent, her right leg extended behind her. Her hands placed just above her bent left knee. Her groin stretching. I gazed open mouthed, enthralled, suffused with the realisation that there was nothing comparable to the beauty of a woman; an attraction that was sticky, and prickling, but also, in this yard where proud horses used to prance and neigh, was noble, animal, aesthetic. The beauty of *this* woman. What an incredible coincidence that was! That my aunt was possibly the most divine woman in the world. I felt what I could only identify as happiness, in my swooning heart, my melting bones. I gazed, enraptured.

By the time I got back inside, my parents were up, and along with Uncle Jonny and Auntie Gwen and Melony, had joined my grandparents at the dining-room table. Everyone had assumed the same seats as the night before, gaps between them.

'*Kids* getting up already, are we?' Uncle Jonny boomed at me. 'This is breakfast, not lunch, you know.'

'Been up hours,' I mumbled.

'Believe him, Jonny,' Dad said, his downtrodden tone suggesting that what his brother should realise was that a child getting up too early was even less agreeable than twins who got up too late.

The air was yeasty with the smell of freshly baked bread, a loaf of which had just emerged from the Aga. Grandma kneaded dough last thing each evening, always using slightly different quantities from the day before, and it was always the tastiest, chewiest bread you ever had. Even though Grandma let Bronwen do increasing amounts of cooking, there was still magic in those gnarled and wrinkled fingers. The bread was so good most people didn't even toast it for breakfast. Steam rose when Auntie Gwen cut it; butter melted; we helped ourselves to Grandma's home-made jam. Raspberry, plum. Crab apple and greengage jellies.

Not that Grandma ate any herself. 'You're losing weight, Ma,' Uncle Jonny told her, but she dismissed him with a wave of her hand, and sipped her tea.

Outside, the bird feeders were besieged by grateful posses: blue tits, great tits, coal tits, a couple of nuthatches, a greenfinch. A robin hovered, and pecked up seeds that had fallen to the ground.

Grandpa had given me a book of birds with beautiful coloured drawings, and helped me to identify them. In the summer a pied wagtail nestled under the eaves of the stables. Swallows and house martins swirled about, while starlings strutted on the ground. A wood pigeon had a nest in the sycamore tree from whose branch the swings hung. It was a summer of white lilac.

'A great spotted woodpecker pays us regular visits,' Grandpa explained to Melony. 'Next time he deigns to, I'll let you –'

'Leonard,' Grandma interrupted, from the opposite end of the table. 'The children are here, now's as good a time as any to tell them.'

'The sooner the better,' Grandpa agreed.

People stopped eating, prepared for a surprise announcement, no idea what to expect. A feeling of dread spread tangible as some indoor mist over the table.

Grandma cleared her throat. 'We asked you all to come here this Christmas,' she said, 'for one reason.' She said no more, but looked to Grandpa, and nodded – whether deferring to him, or rather ordering him to speak, it was impossible to tell.

Grandpa coughed, swallowed, and said, 'Your mother believes the world is doomed.'

There was a pause, before everyone's head turned back as Grandma, as if accepting the return volley, said, 'Well, of course it is. That's perfectly obvious. But the reason we had you here is to sort out the furniture.'

My father, uncle and aunt looked quizzically from one to another.

'The last thing we want,' Grandma said, 'is for our children to squabble over their inheritance. Leonard's sorted out the money, of course. What you do with the property's up to you to decide when the time comes, although I believe Jonny's got some ideas.'

'What does any of this have to do with the end of the world?' my father asked. Mum was sitting across from me, next to Grandpa, at the diagonally opposite end of the table from Dad. I saw her glance at him, their eyes meet. 'Where's the logic?' he asked.

'Don't argue with Ma,' said Uncle Jonny.

Auntie Gwen was shaking her head. 'You need the house, you need the furniture,' she said. 'As for a time when you don't need it, I don't want to think about it.'

Grandma screwed up her face. 'Don't get sentimental, Gwen, for God's sake. All we're talking about are objects.'

Grandpa, meanwhile, turned round and reached for a pad on the dresser behind him.

'What your father has there,' Grandma explained, 'are coloured stickers. Red ones for Jonny, blue for Rodney, yellow for Gwen. It's all very simple.'

'There are sixty pieces of furniture of any value in this house,' Grandpa continued, as if they'd rehearsed alternate lines of dialogue. 'Here's a copy of the list of those items for each of you.'

'I want you to choose the thirty items you most want,' said Grandma, 'and put your coloured sticker on both the item of furniture *and* beside its name on the list. In addition, I want you to prioritise: write the number 1 on the stickers of your ten favourite pieces, number 2 on the next ten, and number 3 on those you like the least.'

'Amongst those we like the most,' said Dad.

'Is that quite clear?' Grandma asked.

I don't know what Melony made of all this. Auntie Gwen had been shaking her head the whole time Grandma was speaking. 'This is a macabre plan,' she said, standing up. 'It's a morbid conversation. I don't want any part of it.'

'Oh, don't be a bloody idiot,' Jonny told her. 'Sit down. What's wrong with you?'

Gwen neither sat back down nor left the table, but stood there, looking bemused.

'What happens to the lists?' Dad asked.

'We'll make copies,' Grandma said. 'Leonard's got a colour camera thing downstairs.'

'Scanner,' Grandpa nodded.

'You can each take a copy home, and we'll send one to the solicitors. And then,' she said, turning to Auntie Gwen, 'you can forget *all* about it.'

No one spoke for a moment, until, to my surprise, my mother said, 'Rosemary'. Turning to Grandpa, she said, 'Leonard'. And back to Grandma, 'What a really intelligent and thoughtful idea. I think it's brilliant, and next time I see my parents I'm going to suggest they consider doing the exact same thing.'

Grandma didn't smile, exactly, but she made a sound, neither a grunt nor a hum but an amalgam of the two: she had no need of Mum's approval, but was happy to accept it – although, one should understand, she very much doubted whether her daughter-in-law's family had sixty antique pieces of furniture in any way comparable to the collection in this house.

Mum's positive appreciation did, though, get discussion going. Uncle Jonny said he reckoned it was partly having nothing concrete from her own past that had inspired Lorna to take up interior design, both of their own house and others; Dad said he'd put stickers on things if that's what his parents wanted.

I followed the conversation for a while, then my attention strayed to my grandmother. Unnoticed, she'd dropped off to sleep. Looking at her, sat in her chair, eyes closed, I had the sudden impression that her body was run on electricity, and that her energy source had become erratic, was being used up too fast, like a faulty battery.

2

My cousins eventually traipsed downstairs, looking worn out by the extra sleep they'd inflicted upon themselves. Having eaten her breakfast, Sidney slumped on a sofa with a new book. Holly claimed her sister was revising, but I doubted it: she never took notes, for one thing; and she read too fast; and anyway it looked more like pleasure, a dismal addiction, than duty.

Holly said she'd catch up with me outside. By the open boot of Uncle Jonny's rhino-like vehicle Grandpa was showing the twins how to press a shotgun against your shoulder, to absorb the kick; Xan and Baz were going Christmas shooting too, for the first time. 'Ready to be bloodied, are we?' their father declared.

I wasn't envious. Grandpa had taken me out once. I hit a rabbit, but failed to kill it outright. We came up and found it lying on its side, twitching, blood seeping from its mouth. Grandpa picked up a fallen branch and finished the poor creature off with a single club to the neck. 'Put it out of its misery,' he said. All I could think of was that a living animal was now lifeless, because of me. It wasn't squeamishness, exactly; I was less bothered by blood than revolted at my having extinguished an animate being, and I declined further invitations to go shooting thereafter.

The high pressure continued: beneath a light-grey sky, an incredible stillness. As if everything was in a state of suspension;

of perfect poise. 'The calm before the storm,' my father had said at breakfast, with his customary life-affirming optimism. There wasn't the slightest murmur of a breeze. I thought of one of those ancient maps where a windy terrain is indicated by a man – a wind God? – blowing a cloud across the landscape. It seemed to me that this God was asleep. I could hear sounds from far away, across the valley: the cawing of crows; a dog barking. Smoke rose from the chimneys of isolated homesteads. The smell of damp woodsmoke emanated from Jockie's bonfire.

The garage was at the end of the stables. I went in and sat on Grandpa's quad bike, waiting for Holly. The air inside was fumey with the smell of petrol, metal, hot oil cooled down. A faint odour of grass. Outside, Uncle Jonny was now on his mobile phone, pacing about the yard, nearer to me than to the others beside his car, just coming into earshot.

'Yes, of course,' he was saying. 'Couldn't agree more.' There were pauses between phrases, as Jonny moved closer to the garage. 'I'll be glad to give whatever assurances you require, of course.' His head was bent, his body in a fixed posture, being moved stiffly around by his legs. 'Shall we say by the twentieth? I see. Of course, but the tenth, I mean, it's cutting it a little fine, I'd have thought. I assumed you'd extend the loan without . . . No, no, I quite understand. Look, let's talk after Christmas. Yes. Really? Good for you. I'm just taking my boys shooting, actually. Enjoy the holiday.'

Uncle Jonny lowered the mobile from his ear and, staring at it, said softly, 'Fuck.' He shook his head and said, more loudly, 'Fuck *you*, arsehole.' He put the phone into the right-hand pocket of his jacket and pulled a different one out of the left. He pressed a single button before raising it to his ear. He was now standing almost in the side doorway of the garage, looking out.

'It's me,' he said. 'Here it is. You've got until the eighth. If I don't have the interest by the tenth, we're fucked. Yeah, yeah, I know, he thinks he's the dog's bollocks.' In contrast to the previous conversation, Uncle Jonny was now animated; although standing still, he gestured with his free hand, nodded his head as if for emphasis to the listener on the other end of the line. 'You never should have shown him the figures, you fucking muppet, of course he's being a cunt. So would I. No. Look, I don't want to hear it, all right? What's on paper doesn't mean fuck. Do you not get it? It's liquidate or die now.'

I'd never heard my uncle – nor any other adult outside movies – speak like this; with this casual, obscene vehemence. It was like a different person, speaking a different language. No, it was like the true animal beneath the civilised veneer – a superficial skin that most people were too timid ever to divest themselves of. My uncle was able and willing to.

'At least the bastard will accept property as well as cash,' he said. 'I can raise a Bernie's worth here. You unfreeze capital, I'll get what title deeds I can on the table. I don't give a fuck if it's Christmas. Santa Claus isn't going to help us, you twat. Get to work.'

Uncle Jonny put the mobile phone back in his left-hand pocket, turned around, stepped into the doorway, and stared straight at me. With the light from outside all around him, I couldn't make out the features of his face: he was simply a dark silhouette. He didn't say anything. He must have been staring at me. At last he spoke. 'You have to take risks. Don't be a loser, Theo.' His voice was almost back to normal. 'You have to cover those risks as best you can. Protect yourself. Protect your family. You don't *have* to be poor. It's your father's choice. *You* don't have to make the same choice.'

He turned and walked across the yard. Halfway to the others he called to them, 'We all set? Got those useless gundogs of yours ready, Pa?' They piled into their paramilitary-style vehicle, and took off down the drive.

I knew that my parents, and thus myself, were not poor, exactly, but nor were we rich. When she opened the *Oxford Times* my mother always went straight to the Property section, and would interrupt my father trying to read the news section with his Friday gin and tonic to show him some large Victorian house for sale, nearer the centre of town. They'd not moved house since before I was born and had no plans to; this property envy was just one of my mother's foibles which neither my father nor myself took seriously. I'd never considered ourselves impoverished. There were plenty of kids at school from poorer homes than mine, from the Cutteslowe and Marston estates – even if they generally had more cash to flash around than I did – and I tended to compare my lot to theirs rather than the few children I knew who went to private schools in the city. But to my entrepreneur uncle, his older brother's family must have seemed positively deprived. I knew full well, by that time in my life, that such considerations are relative. But what I could not deny was that there was something deeply exciting about the way my uncle had spoken on the phone, and then to me. He possessed some kind of energy I'd not come across before, which I guessed was to do with power over others, exerted for the sake of money.

Grandma walked slowly across the yard, using a stick, beside Jockie. 'Bring some potatoes inside,' she said. 'Enough for the week.'

'I'll use the barrow,' Jockie informed her.

'You're getting weak,' Grandma told him. 'Getting old.'

'I'll never be as old as you,' he replied.

They always spoke like this, bickering with each other. They had the strangest relationship. Mistress and servant, lifelong friends, locked together in feudal enmity.

'I thought I told you not to come today.'

'We're behind with pruning, ain't it?'

'It's winter.'

'Been too bloody mild.'

'You're only here for the money.'

'Your husband can afford it.'

It was well known that Jockie wouldn't take orders from Grandpa. 'He's getting chippy with Leonard again,' Grandma would say with some glee. Mostly, her gardener just got on with whatever he thought needed doing. Grandma would interrupt and tell him to do something else, out of a sort of obligation to exert her authority, and he'd listen to what she had to say and then go back to whatever he was doing before.

Holly and I spent the morning exploring. I wanted to show her my favourite places. The first was Grandpa's workshop in the coach house, which you reached – unless its big double doors were open – through a side door. There were shelves along all the brick walls, shelves that had once been floorboards in rooms in the house, replaced fifty years ago. Arrayed upon them were jam-jars and tins filled with all manner of screws, nails, rivets and hinges; washers and plugs, bolts, switches. Unlike in Grandpa's geological mini-museuem, there were no labels here to identify the size or gauge of hardware. Lengths of rope and string, coils of wire, differing thicknesses of electrical flex. Running right along the whitewashed back wall was a long, thick slab of wood, the workbench, above which hung every imaginable tool, over its felt-pen outline. Saws, hammers, spanners. Screwdrivers, chisels, pliers.

We looked through cans, at parts we could not identify of machines we were unable to imagine. There were implements that were broken and which Grandpa was planning to get around to mending, or had tried to fix and failed to; a large lock whose back had been removed, and whose parts lay all jumbled in a little heap inside; an ancient electrical appliance whose wires and springs spilled out like the entrails of some abandoned dissection.

'Amazing, isn't it?' I asked Holly.

'What is?' she asked.

'You know,' I said. 'All this.'

'All what?' she said.

I thought it was self-evident, and was at a loss to explain.

'All these bits and pieces,' I said, waving my arms around to indicate the totality of objects in tins and jars all around the workshop. 'They all fitted into something once, and Grandpa's kept hold of them, because any one of them could come in useful again one day. Except they won't, because things aren't made like that any more, of replaceable parts: something breaks, you bin it and buy a new one. Grandpa wouldn't know how to fix a modern radio, or hairdryer, or electric drill. It's kind of, I don't know, sad, isn't it?'

Holly shrugged. She didn't really get what I was on about, and after a while neither did I. What did impress her was that at one end of the workbench were paintbrushes; containers of putty, white spirit, turps. On the shelves above were cans of paint with stickers, on which were written the room they'd adorned, kept for touching up. Grandpa or Jockie or someone must have tested colours on the table, or maybe tried to work excess paint off a brush: layers of different colours, vintages and types of paint had created a thick impasto that she gazed at for a while. 'A collaboration between Jackson Pollock and Howard Hodgkin,' she said. Seeing my puzzlement – neither of my parents were much into visual arts; nor was I – she said, 'Art's my best subject. Our school's got Art specialist status.'

She drew her small camera out of the pocket of her hoodie, and took pictures.

The smell of turpentine, and linseed oil, entered one's nostrils. Holly reached up and brought down a bell that hung on the wall. 'I wonder what this is for?' she asked.

'It was Grandpa's grandfather's. He was a shepherd.' Grandpa had told me about him. 'He always had a hand-reared lamb, which became the leading sheep: it would follow him, and the rest of the flock would follow it, or rather they'd follow the sound of the bell around its neck. He could walk in front of the flock, open gates, lead the way. His dogs would follow behind, rounding up stragglers.'

'I didn't know about the shepherd,' Holly said.

'Grandpa said his earliest memory is of picking acorns in the autumn for his grandfather's pig.'

'Until yesterday, I thought he was always wealthy.'

I shook my head. 'He had nothing,' I told her. 'He made it all himself.'

3

Lunch was a mishmash of a meal, concocted by various members of the family. Melony and Holly prepared a salad, while I made sure everyone witnessed me making houmous in Grandma's Kenwood liquidiser, and understood that I was adding ingredients from memory: one tin of chick peas; half a jar of tahini; two cloves of garlic, crushed; the juice of one lemon; water from the chick peas, to achieve a desired consistency, and soy sauce to taste.

'I prefer not to follow a recipe,' I explained to Holly. 'I'm more of an intuitive cook, really.' She was deeply impressed, I could tell.

A large block of cheddar and another of Stilton joined the shoulder of ham on the counter.

Just as we sat calmly, quietly tucking in, we heard loud excited voices, doors banging. Grandpa, Uncle Jonny and the twins came striding noisily in, the dogs weaving around their legs. Xan and Baz each held up a rabbit by its hind legs; each boy had an identical, proud grin on his face.

'I don't want blood on my kitchen tiles!' Grandma exclaimed. 'Hang them in the scullery, Leonard.'

'The boys just wanted to show you,' Grandpa told her.

'Yes, yes, very good,' Grandma said. 'Now go and wash your hands and be so good as to join us for lunch.'

If the four hunters had expected cheering to greet their heroic return, they didn't look crestfallen by its absence; they were too wrapped up in their shared exertions. When they'd left the room, Grandma said, *sotto voce*, wrinkling her nose dismissively, 'Of course, it's not *real* hunting.'

When they returned and joined us at the table, the twins told how they'd both bagged their quarry within ten minutes of leaving the car.

'The poor bunnies were fast asleep,' Uncle Jonny said. 'We were practically upon them, could have knocked the little blighters on the head with the tip of the gun barrel as easily as shot them.'

'Father's upset,' said Xan, 'because he didn't pop a pheasant.'

'Kept missing,' Baz agreed.

'We only came home when he ran out of cartridges.'

'Ho, ho,' Uncle Jonny said, which was his personal alternative to laughing, something he never did; he just acknowledged other people's remarks. 'Ho, ho. I blame Pa's bloody dogs. They blundered around in the undergrowth, alerting all the game to our presence.'

Grandpa didn't say anything. He just sat there at the head of the table, basking in the recounting of the morning's expedition, and in the rare gathered company of his offspring.

Dessert was a fruit salad Mum and Gwen had put together, with a choice of yoghurt or crème fraîche to go with it, and there were trays of dried dates and crystallised ginger.

My father had avoided preparing anything, as usual; he'd been in the TV area, or what had become the reading area, slumped in a chair across the room from Sid, each lost in their own world, oblivious to the rest of us working our fingers to the bone, as Grandma put it, getting their lunch ready for them. They didn't appear to hear a word.

The truth was that my father was smarter, and wilier, than people gave him credit for. He pretended to be all clumsy and vague and forgetful, but he didn't fool me. Like when Mum moaned about doing most of the cooking, he'd wait until people were coming to dinner and insist on taking responsibility. He'd waste all morning shopping for precise ingredients, then spend the afternoon in the kitchen ruining the meal. He'd be cursing loudly in there, while I was helping Mum hand round alcohol and olives, and you could tell it gave the impression to their guests that he'd been forced somewhat against his will to prepare their food. There was always at least one noisy breakage. Eventually he'd call everyone to the table and serve up one dish underdone, another one burned. The mashed potato was lumpy, the joint was still half-raw or the supposedly al dente pasta was soft.

Most adults, I gathered, had what they called a signature dish, a particular delicious meal they could cook. My father had signature dishes of his own: meals that were legendary for their awfulness. They were brought up in conversation by his and Mum's friends for years afterwards. 'Remember Rod's broad bean pasta? Or what about the time he gave us food poisoning with that uncooked salmon?' The memories were regurgitated, accompanied by grimaces and laughter. They loved him for it. And the thing you wouldn't believe unless you saw it with your own eyes was that Mum fell for it, too. She and Dad would laugh about each travesty of a meal after the guests had gone home, and for days afterwards.

And my father would say things like, 'I just don't get how it's possible to cook more than two dishes and serve them at the same time. I can't see how it's possible, darling, and sometimes you serve *six*!'

My mother would accept the compliment and have a pleasant chuckle every time she kicked him out of the kitchen. 'I'm not letting *you* in here.' Until six months later she'd start moaning about always having to do the cooking and what was wrong with the men in this house?

The thing was, every now and then Mum would go away, to a conference or on one of her girlfriends' walking weekends, and Dad would knock me and him up decent grub – or 'tucker,' as he called it – without ever breaking anything, or swearing. Whereas my mother, it seemed to me, was not as smart as she – and everyone else – thought she was. But she bossed people around at work, and gave lectures to hundreds of students, and Dad was always telling her how clever she was, and she believed it.

'Amy takes care of our money,' he'd tell people. 'I haven't the brains for it.'

'I couldn't trust Rod with the bills,' Mum would say. 'He hasn't a clue.'

But take Scrabble. I'd been playing with my parents for a while by then, occasionally, just to humour them. And even I'd beaten Mum, when I had decent letters. But she was always outraged if Dad was winning, like she couldn't believe it, and he'd say, 'Pure luck, darling. I'm so sorry. What are the odds of getting a Z on the double-letter of the triple-word score, with a seven-letter word? Pure fluke.' But the thing was, you see, they kept a little old notebook in the Scrabble box to write the scores in, and one rainy day I checked back through them. They must have been playing Scrabble together for years. Sometimes another one or two people played – what thrilling dinner parties those must have been – usually it was just the two of them. I totalled the results. Dad led Mum by a hundred and seventy-three games to sixty-one.

I'd not drawn Mum's attention to this, nor had I any intention of doing so.

Grandpa was asking Melony about her work. She was a nurse, or at least she used to be. Now she seemed to be something else. He asked her if she'd ever worked in a hospice — I don't know why — and it turned out she'd been a nurse at Sobell House in Oxford. She told Grandpa a story of how Doctor So-and-so had this private patient, and requested that Melony find her a single room.

'I was so determined not to give her preferential treatment that even though one happened to be free, I moved another patient out of the four-bed ward and into the room.' She shook her head. Melony spoke quietly, just loud enough for Grandpa to hear, although by straining hard and leaning a little across Sid, who was talking to Aunt Lorna next to her, I was just about able to as well.

'The result was that the woman I'd moved was miserable. In the last days of her life. She hated being alone, cut off, from the small community she'd just joined.'

'What about the private patient?' Grandpa asked.

Melony made a wry shrug. 'She integrated immediately in the ward, and was very happy there.'

Myself, I'd barely said a word to Melony. Two shy people are a poor combination. Shy people may resent loud and insensitive boors, but also appreciate the fact that they don't notice their shyness; it means they can ignore it themselves. Whereas you know that another shy person is acutely aware of your every hesitation and anxiety.

Seated in the middle, between Sid and Holly, I could sweep the entire company. Aunt Lorna, fortunately, was blocked by Sid: since this morning, I'd avoided looking at her, afraid that if I did so I might faint. At the end of the table to my right, Uncle Jonny seemed to be inviting his brother and sister to join him on a Christmas Eve pub crawl. 'Catch up with one or two of the old crowd,' he said. 'Bound to be there.'

Dad frowned. 'I'm not really sure,' he said.

'I think I'll stay here with Melony,' said Auntie Gwen.

'Bring her,' Jonny said, with a sort of exasperated shrug. 'It's the twenty-first bloody century, Gwen.'

My aunt screwed up her nose as if to indicate her scepticism at this proposition. 'Round here?'

'Maybe Pa would like to come,' Uncle Jonny wondered aloud.

'Leonard?' Grandma said, loudly. 'Your father's never been in a public house in his entire *life*. Why on earth would he start now?'

The twins, meanwhile, were conferring behind my mother's back. 'Why don't you two ask to get down?' she told them. Xan leaned towards her and whispered something in her ear. 'Oh, I don't know,' Mum said.

'But you have to announce it,' Xan said.

'It's a challenge,' said Baz. 'Even if it is a stupid one.'

Mum took a deep breath and sighed loudly, alerting everyone around the table to pay attention. 'We've been offered a challenge by these two and their parents, apparently: the Hampstead Cannons challenge the rest of the family to a game of football in the riding school this afternoon. Kick-off two-thirty.'

I added up the likely members of their opposition, discounting only my grandparents.

'It's a ridiculous challenge,' Baz told Sid. 'Best to humour my brother, everyone. He's got some kind of Tension Deficit Disorder.'

Xan scanned us around the table, bug-eyed, leering with gritted teeth. 'Yes,' he said. 'I'm very tense.'

'Or not tense enough,' Baz said.

'Exactly,' Xan agreed.

'There are four of you and six of us,' I told him.

'Quality not quantity,' Xan said.

'Seven, actually,' said Baz.

'Theo forgot to count himself,' said Xan.

'He would,' Baz reckoned.

I stared from one to the other of the twins, forgetting for a moment that a dozen people were watching. 'Are you ready to be merked?' I asked.

4

My cousin Sidney had the ability like a burglar to enter or exit a room unseen. You never noticed her leave: one moment she was there, curled up on the sofa, the next time you looked she was gone, leaving behind only the indentation of her boney frame in the cushions and an opened, face-down book. Often you didn't notice her absence, to be honest, so diffident and insubstantial was her presence, and you'd be mildly surprised to come across her in a different room curled up in a chair, with a different book, but always with the same empty, zombified expression.

'Reminds me of myself,' my father remarked, somehow approving and plaintive both at once. And with a regretful glance in my direction.

Observing Sid gave one the impression that perhaps reading required a strange courage: that opening a book exposed you to some invisible substance within, lurking between the words, like radium, that sapped your vitality. All the reading Sid did exhausted her. Her only fear, she said, was that she'd not brought enough books with her and would run out before it was time to go back to London. I assured her that Grandpa's library was extensive, but she didn't appear to have visited it, and wasn't convinced. 'I've read most of the classics,' she told me.

Sid joined in the football match we played that Christmas Eve afternoon, however, as did everyone else. And though I may find it painful, I shall do my best to describe it.

The day remained mild, and still, though the sky above the valley darkened a little, to a deeper grey. It was the kind of day when there's rain in the air, but it falls so lightly that you have to concentrate to actually perceive its existence: the idea of rain seemed to present itself to one's mind. I looked at my clothes and saw tiny beads of moisture, condensing out of the air, it appeared, rather than falling from the sky. Miniscule drops stained the paving stones as we crossed the patio.

The opposition were already on the pitch. Baz had his hands in his trouser pockets, and was staring into space. Xan, playing keepy-uppy with a yellow and purple Premiership football, was dressed in a blue Chelsea kit, with DECO printed on the back. Aunt Lorna was in her black running gear. Our team shuffled across the yard dressed in our normal clothes. At least Uncle Jonny was in his usual jeans and open-necked shirt. 'If he's so rich,' I asked Holly, 'why does he wear cheap gear?'

'Haven't you seen the labels?' she whispered back. 'Prada. Roberto Cavalli. Those jeans cost a thousand squids.'

'What could you have here?' Aunt Lorna was asking Uncle Jonny. 'A swimming pool?' The square-shaped riding school had a sandy surface, which Xan claimed would suit his family's total football, and he'd set goals using cones for posts in two opposite corners, explaining that otherwise the goals would be too close together. I agreed, and so the square riding school was transformed into a diamond-shaped football pitch.

Xan was a neat and skilful player, with quick feet, fond of step-overs and dragbacks; his favoured trick was to see how long he could stand over a motionless ball, feinting one way or the other, pretending to kick it but holding back, before eventually looking in one direction and passing it in quite another. I had to admit that despite being smaller, and a year younger, he and I were equally matched.

The funny thing was that his brother was useless. It must have been the only interest the twins didn't share. Baz spent the entire match in goal, hiding inside a hooded anorak, shod in a pair of Grandpa's wellies. Of the few shots we got on target he saved the ones that hit him, and failed to save any that, to Xan's annoyance, rolled by on either side. Baz's one useful contribution was, having climbed through the poles surrounding the school to retrieve a ball, to then boot it out of his hands – ignoring the legal requirements of a goal-kick or centre – and send it sailing towards the other end, the opposite diagonal, of the pitch, and the opposition goal, whose custodian was my mother: although generally as incompetent as Baz, if the ball came towards her she did at least make an effort to pick it up.

Uncle Jonny played in defence for the London Cannons, Aunt Lorna up front, while Xan patrolled the middle. They had a spine to their team, and nothing else. We, on the other hand, were shapeless. I stuck close to Xan. The south London women – Gwen, Melony, Sid and Holly – wandered around the riding school according to impulses of their own, flitting in and out of the action. My father, though he had no idea how to play it, was a connoisseur of the beautiful game. He stood off to one side, an amused grin on his face, occasionally collecting a stray pass but chiefly issuing sardonic advice to all and sundry. Whenever Baz in goal readied himself to boot the ball upfield Dad pre-empted him, calling out, 'Load it!' Chuckling to himself. 'Launch it!'

* * *

Our players were hopeless. Aunt Gwen peered through her large spectacles at the bodies revolving around her, apparently unable to make sense of their movement. Melony flattered to deceive: she was able to bring the ball under control, but couldn't work out what to do with it next, dwelling on it until one of our opponents came and took it off her, or else, with Dad yelling ironically, 'Get rid! Lump it!' toe-poking it aimlessly forward.

Holly was reasonably fit and limber. Sidney, on the other hand, although surprisingly energetic, prised from the stupor of her reading and into the fray, was utterly unco-ordinated. All four of her thin limbs, accustomed to being folded up in a chair, when let loose seemed to operate disconnected from each other; each one looked like it wanted to assist its owner to flap in a different direction from all the others. In addition, the perfectly round leather globe she was required to do something with was obviously for Sid a both startling and hilarious proposition. It was as if the ball were alive, and bounced in an unpredictable manner, because whenever it came towards Sidney she giggled, nervously and loudly, and tried to overcome her warring arms and legs and kick it, in any direction at all. Sid's panic created an optical illusion: the ball did indeed look, around her, like one of those joke balls that bounce any and which way.

'Put it in the mixer!' Dad shouted.

The trouble was that our opponents were not quite so hopeless. Uncle Jonny, though lacking finesse, was a battering ram who made no allowance for age, gender or size. He shoulder-barged Melony out of the way and blocked Holly with a tackle that sent her flying in the sand.

Aunt Lorna was – unfortunately – a revelation. Not only did she not have to stop running to get her breath back, as all our players did, she was also fast. More than that, though, she knew how to play football: was able to anticipate the flight of the ball, or dummy and let the ball run past her marker so that she could carry on towards goal unimpeded. As Xan and I cancelled each other out in midfield I was obliged to witness the rest of the game unfold: Uncle Jonny bullied our attackers out of the way; Baz punted the ball forward for his mother to outwit or outpace our defenders, and help herself to three goals, before Jonny strode forward and had a pop himself, booting the ball at our goal as hard as he could. It smacked Mum full in the face, and as we gathered around her, lying in the sand, someone announced, mercifully, 'Half-time.'

I rearranged things for the second half. With my mother sitting on the poles at the side of the school, one cheek all red, cheering us on, Auntie Gwen went in goal. Unable to make out clearly what was going on in front of her, she came out bravely and made some crucial, entirely fortuitous blocks. I persuaded my father to hang around in defence, along with Melony, and stuck Sid up front in the hope that she might distract Uncle Jonny enough to give Holly the opportunity of a shot or two. For myself, I would have liked nothing more than to man-mark my Aunt Lorna – sticking close as an Italian defender, a sly shadow, one hand tugging her shirt, the other gripping her arm – but I knew it would be a suicidal manoeuvre, that Xan would waltz around our other players and gorge himself on goals.

I stuck to my role, and at first our tactics worked. From a goal-kick, Gwen gave the ball to Melony, who, under orders from Dad to 'Hoof it!', kicked it past Xan and myself, towards Sid, who tried desperately to bring this ungovernable missile under control, giggling and shrieking, even as it bobbled erratically around her shins. Uncle Jonny came steaming in, but was so confused by Sid's chaotic dance that he missed her entirely and stumbled over himself, leaving Holly to get the ball and, for once, direct it between Baz's immobile frame and the post.

That was the extent of our good fortune. Our opponents scored twice more, once through Xan, who lost his marker – myself – tapped in at the far post and set off on a celebration that consisted of gliding and veering in between our team's players with one arm outstretched like a bird's wing and the other cupped to his ear, taunting us.

At this point Dad consulted his watch and said, 'It's after three-thirty and getting dark. Next goal's the winner.'

You might have thought he'd declared Christmas to have been cancelled, and there would be no presents, specifically not for twins, such was Xan's outrage.

'That is so *totally* not fair,' he screamed, tears in his eyes at the injustice of the proposal.

'Quite so,' Jonny agreed. 'Don't be ridiculous, Rod.'

'It's only a game,' our blind but not deaf goalkeeper Auntie Gwen called out.

'Precisely,' Uncle Jonny responded. 'Like life itself. Something you've never understood.'

'You can't win!' Xan howled at me. 'You're four goals behind!'

'Whatever,' I shrugged, feeling my way towards a certain moral superiority. 'I'm easy.'

'We're not bothered either way,' Dad said.

'You never bloody are,' Jonny agreed.

'Why don't we call it a draw and go in for tea?' Mum

suggested from the sideline, which made our opponents even more furious.

'You can't stop now!' Xan shrieked, turning purple with indignation.

Even Aunt Lorna joined in, telling Melony with an elegant shrug of her shoulders, 'If you play, you have to play to win.'

In the end it was agreed that the next goal would be the last one, but that the score remained five-one. We couldn't even salvage much pride. Our opponents needn't have worried: we didn't salvage any. We pressed forward briefly, and Holly kicked the ball weakly towards their goal. It came to rest at Baz's feet. He bent down and picked it up.

'Put some snow on it!' Dad yelled, and Baz obliged with his longest punt of the day. The ball flew over everyone's heads, coming to an eventual rest a few yards from our goal. Gwen peered blindly out. I called to her to step forward and pick it up, but she stayed rooted to her line.

Aunt Lorna and our defenders meanwhile gave chase. It was no contest. I watched helplessly – Xan beside me saying under his breath, 'Go on, Mum. Go on,' – as she outstripped first my poor gasping father, then struggling Melony, who, to my and probably everyone else's surprise, as Lorna drew away from her, threw out a hand to try and pull her back. She missed and, grabbing only air, floundered. Aunt Lorna reached the ball alone, calmly tapped it past Gwen, and with arms aloft turned to accept the congratulations of her teammates.

'The winner!' Xan exclaimed, as if he'd agreed to Dad's proposal, and he and his father rushed to embrace Aunt Lorna. I watched them, filled with bitterness. How I would have liked to run over and embrace her, too.

Baz wandered up behind me. 'Thank God that's over,' he said. 'Who won, anyway?'

As we strolled back across the yard – 'to tea and hot buttered crumpets, I trust,' said Mum – Uncle Jonny told Dad that his trouble was that he didn't know the difference between art and sport. 'You think that unless the game's beautiful, it's worthless.'

The two adult brothers walked side by side. I flanked my father, Xan his. 'Sport,' Dad said, 'is art, with the addition of competition.'

'Nonsense,' said Jonny. 'You see, that's where you're completely wrong. Sport evolved from hunting, and tribal fighting. It's war, without violence.'

'Or in your case,' Dad said, nodding towards Holly, limping ahead of us, 'a modest level of violence.'

'War without death,' said Jonny. 'That's what sport is. And thanks to your warrior mother,' he added, turning to Xan, 'we won the bloody battle.' At which father and son high-fived.

5

'Don't take it too hard, old son.' I'd descended to my grandfather's study to escape Xan's crowing, our women's sympathy. He did his best to console me. 'Sounds like you never had a chance.' The dogs, too, offered their support. Leda had come to me, tail wagging, when I entered the room; Sel was more surreptitious, and I didn't notice her until I realised that she must have sidled up and nuzzled against me, and that for some while now I'd been stroking her neck with my hand.

'Xan issued that challenge as if it was daring and brave,' I moaned. 'When it was just a way of making sure he was on the winning team.'

'People are rarely who or what they seem,' Grandpa said. 'I'm afraid you'll need to be prepared for this sort of skulduggery.'

It occurred to me then, with the force of revelation, that Xan, and his father, were Grandpa's offspring just as much as Dad and I were. He'd made his fortune from nothing. Perhaps he was capable of skulduggery himself.

'Treat people as you find them,' my grandfather advised. 'I'd never con a man,' he assured me. 'But I'm damned if I'll let anyone con me.'

Grandpa turned his attention back to the book he was reading, shifting his gaze from above to through the rims of his half-moon spectacles. He was sitting in a low, old armchair. It was covered in a rug which had slipped and rucked beneath his body, revealing threadbare patches on the upholstered arms. A column of books rose from the ground on either side of the chair; a further scattering on the coffee table in front of him. A large notebook lay open on his lap. On the walls behind and around him the bookshelves were crammed: any space between the tops of books and the shelf above was filled with books lying on their sides. My grandfather, as I indicated earlier, was not a tall man, and he looked even smaller in the comfortable armchair. It was easy to imagine that he was being gradually absorbed, swallowed up, by his library.

My grandfather was working on a history of the border country between England and Wales, 'this disputed land', as he called it, quoting from one of his many sources. The resulting book would be 'the definitive account', his son, my father, reckoned – with almost as much filial affection in his voice, I detected, as his customary scepticism. After a career making money Grandpa had determined, upon retirement ten years earlier, to immerse himself in the history of the region. He assumed his book would be completed within a year or two. The reason it had taken so long, he explained to me, was that he kept digging further and further back in time, ever wider in place – deep into Wales, up and down Offa's Dyke – and into an increasing variety of subjects, from geology to architecture; from archaeology to flora and fauna to military dress to climate change to animal husbandry to local government to . . . It was a dizzying project. 'I'm like a toddler gathering sheep,' my grandfather told me. He'd spend a morning with an old hill farmer, listening to memories of Edwardian grandparents, and the afternoon with members of the Friends of the Shropshire Archives discussing the Shropshire Enlightenment.

'Now I can see,' he'd memorably proclaimed, in the depth of his absorption, at the height of his frustration, 'why academics restrict themselves to such stultifyingly limited areas of research.'

'Thanks for that generous acknowledgement, Pa,' my father had replied.

While Grandpa read his latest textbook, occasionally taking a pencil from behind his ear like a carpenter – as if this were manual as much as intellectual labour – and scratching something in the margin, I walked over to the shelf where, in a metre-long space protected from encroachment by heavy wooden bookends, lay a jumble of artefacts my grandfather had collected in his research. Each artefact had an old luggage label attached to it with white cotton, on which was written a description in Grandpa's spidery script.

Before showing these items to Holly, I thought I'd better remind myself of their historical context. There was a pig of lead imprinted with the name of the Emperor Hadrian, which Grandpa had found near the Stiperstones; a Roman coin he'd dug from the hill camp on Nordy Bank; a shard of pottery from the ruins of Viroconium, near Shrewsbury, the fourth largest Roman city in Britain.

After the final withdrawal of the Roman legions in the fifth century, marauding Saxons came in waves crashing on the eastern and southern shores: as they pushed west, so the British warriors withdrew to the Welsh mountains. Grandpa had a Saxon arrowhead, and the tip of a British guerrilla's spear. Our grandfather had become an amateur historian, of a sort that academics like his son and daughter-in-law tended to regard with condescension, but it had engaged him, he said, in a way he'd never imagined, made him see the land around him as composed of layers of human lifetimes as well as of geology. He passed on this sense of engagement to me: I understood that we could experience this life as shallowly or as deeply as we wished. We walked on solid ground, in the company of ghostly companions; and furthermore that ground, this disputed land, might be taken from us as it was taken from others.

The Saxons, in turn, were overcome by Normans, and were themselves pushed west. William the Conqueror settled his most savage Norman knights in the border country, where they became known as the Marcher Lords, holding sway over the territory they were given and any more they could wrest from the Welsh. On Grandpa's shelf were, so he claimed with perhaps, in hindsight, a certain amount of poetic licence, a scrap of chain mail worn by Robert de Say of Clun, and Roger de Lacy of Ludlow's own helmet.

For the next two hundred years Welsh princes swept down from the mountains to do battle with the Marcher Lords, part of a greater Welsh resistance, until in twelve eighty-two Edward I gathered a huge English army and conquered once and for all the wild country. The last prince was David, captured and sentenced to death in Shrewsbury, where he was drawn and quartered. You could feel with a shudder the brutality of that time in the weapon on Grandpa's shelf, a mace, used to mash people's flesh and bones.

Until the Civil War the borders remained comparatively quiet, then, for the next four hundred years. Welsh long-bowmen stood alongside the English launching showers of arrows with which they slaughtered French forces at Crécy, Poitiers, Agincourt. 'With arrowheads like this one, Theo,' my grandfather had told me. 'Feel it in your hand.' The small blob of sharpened metal felt ominously compact and heavy. 'They fell like hail, piercing the armour of the fiercest knights in Europe.'

Some five years into the project, Grandpa understood the enormity of his ambition. 'If I'd only begun it as a young man, devoted my life to that instead of the fruit business,' he told me, his voice trailing off into consideration of what might have been; a life like his son's, after all. From that moment he began gradually restraining his research, working his way back towards something more manageable. 'I intend to publish a monograph on the history of our village next year,' he'd said that summer. 'Perhaps, after that, an essay on this house, and your grandmother's family.'

My grandfather removed his glasses and closed the book he was reading. He got wearily to his feet and carried the notebook to his desk. 'What time is it, old son?' he asked. Before I could answer, the clock on the mantlepiece chimed once, on the half-hour. It was a typical Grandpa trick.

'Sun almost over the yardarm: those dipsomaniacs upstairs will demand their sauce,' he said, taking a pipe from the ashtray on his desk and relighting it with a red-tipped Swan Vesta match. The tobacco in the bowl caught with an audible hiss. Grandpa shook the match and dropped it in the ashtray, and gazed out of the wide window, into the garden. I didn't know anyone else who smoked a pipe; it was a both traditional and exotic practice. The smoke had a pungent acridity I found immensely appealing, and it was to breathe it in that I stood beside my grandfather, looking out. In the moonlight we could just see, above the beech hedge circumvallating the lawn, the tops of trees in the wood beyond the grazing pasture.

'The twins told me,' I said, 'that your wood's like the New Forest, or the Forest of Dean: original English woodland.'

Grandpa laughed, in his own, particular way. A throaty chuckle, made with a warm smile on his face, so that even though he was laughing at you it wasn't done unkindly. The twins had rinsed me, successfully, and he was amused by this success – and hoped that I would be, too.

'It's not true, is it?' I said. 'I didn't think it was.'

'I planted those trees the year my father-in-law died, Theo,' Grandpa said. 'Fifty-two years ago. A year after your grandmother and I were married.' He turned to me and, nodding, said, 'Every single one of them myself. My back aches with the memory.'

'Why didn't you get Jockie to help you?' I asked.

Grandpa smiled. 'I wanted to do it,' he said. He sucked on his pipe. 'The only trouble with Jockie is he can't stop tidying things up.'

I wondered what was wrong with that.

My grandfather gazed into the distance. 'I like a little mess,' he said.

I asked him how long the trees would be here. He sucked on the stem of his pipe and blew smoke from his mouth, its aroma reaching my eager nostrils.

'They survived the great storm of eighty-seven,' he said. 'We're not expecting another one for a couple of hundred years, are we?'

I found my parents in their blue bedroom. Chatting to each other, they didn't notice me slip in. Mum was kneeling on the carpet, wrapping presents. Dad leaned back against a large chest of drawers, breaking off and passing to her short strips of

Sellotape. I lay on my front on one of the beds, feet by the pillows, looking down on them.

'She's got a nice figure, wouldn't you say?' Mum conjectured.

'I really didn't notice,' Dad said.

'I only wonder if it's real. Her breasts seem rather perfect, don't you think?' Mum measured paper, cut out the sizes she needed. 'I can't imagine she ever breastfed those twins.'

'I wouldn't know.'

'Paid some Mapuche wetnurse to do it for her, I wouldn't be surprised.'

Dad stuck bits of tape to his knuckles. It brought to mind for a moment a boxer – a wonderfully inappropriate image for my gentle father. 'I thought you told me she goes to a gym,' he said.

'All the time,' Mum confirmed.

'Well, there you go.'

As he spoke, my father bent his head until it rested on his left shoulder. Then, in slow motion, he gradually leaned his entire torso in that direction. Mum stopped what she was doing. She and I glanced at each other, and both stared at this extraordinary behaviour. It looked like the beginning of some yoga stretching exercise Dad hadn't done for twenty years, and had just remembered. He put out a Sellotape-covered hand to the carpet to support himself as he leaned further.

'Quite amazing,' he said. Mum and I waited for further explanation. He got up to a kneeling position, shuffled on his knees past Mum, took hold of the chair by the dressing table, and turned it over. There, on the base of its seat, was a red sticker, with the number 2 written on it.

'Pa bought me this when I won first prize in a national essay-writing competition,' my father said. 'I was fourteen. "The first in our family with a chair in history," Pa said. And look: my brother's put one of his bloody stickers on it.'

My father hardly ever cursed. The way that he stretched the first consonant, creating an extra syllable, and then put the stress on the second – 'his ber-*ludd*-y stickers' – made me see them as truly blood red.

Mum shook her head. 'Well,' she said, 'at least it's not a first priority.'

'I'd figured the only object I really wanted was my parents' portrait. And one or two of Pa's archaeological finds. But you know what?' Dad said, frowning. 'This needs to be taken seriously. We have to be a bit clever about it.'

Mum and I waited for him to explain.

'We need to work out what we want, and then consider how likely Jonny – or indeed Gwen – are to want the same pieces. We need to gamble. I mean, there are probably one or two things I want that the others can have no possible interest in. In which case we can put them in the third category.'

'I see what you mean,' Mum said. 'Don't waste first or even second choices on what no one else wants. But I mean it should be easy: Jonny appears to have put stickers on what he wants already. Wait for Gwen to do the same.'

My father tapped his skull. 'Good thinking, Amy,' he said. 'But hang on.' Dad paused, took a breath, and sighed. 'You know I wouldn't put it past him to lay a false trail. I really wouldn't.'

The gong rang downstairs. We gathered in the drawing room. The doors of the wood-burning stove were open and the fire crackled and roared. The pile of presents in their different coloured wrapping paper, to which my parents and I now added a further contribution, had grown momentous. It looked like a film studio prop, a representation of family gifts rather than the real thing. It was easy to imagine that inside each package was nothing but an empty brown cardboard box.

Grandpa opened a bottle of champagne, allowing the cork to pop and bounce off the ceiling: he poured it into flutes which the twins passed round. 'Pity Jonny's not here,' he said. 'He'd appreciate this vintage.'

I was just close enough to overhear Aunt Lorna whisper to Melony, 'By ten'o'clock he would drink meths.'

'Where is our dear brother?' Dad asked Gwen.

She leaned towards him. 'Gone to the pub, like he said,' she confided, as if they were all my age still, and covering for the mischievous brother; keeping his escapade out of earshot of their mother. 'Said he'd be back for supper.'

Our grandmother sat in her chair beside the fire. Xan handed her a glass of champagne, saying, 'Try not to drink it too fast, Grandma.'

'Don't be fresh with me, young man,' she told him, and then, raising her head, addressing us all, 'Marvellous news! I've received a new text from Matt on my own mobile. He's arriving tomorrow, as early as he can make it, and he can't *wait* to get here.' My grandmother looked so happy she glowed; because, I supposed, he'd managed to text her directly, without intermediaries.

A second bottle was opened, the cork this time flying at an angle and dropping on Melony's head, for which Grandpa apologised without ceasing to chuckle.

'I thought Mattie was coming to*day*,' Baz said, in a peevish tone.

'He'll come when he's quite ready, thank you very much,' Grandma said. 'As soon as he possibly can.'

I was focussing on people's conversations, partly to keep my gaze from drifting to my aunt, but my head kept turning of its own volition in her direction, and I'd find myself staring at her, and have to wrench my attention away. She wore a tight shirt which had red flowers on it and also gauzy, see-through bits, and black flared trousers, and the same perfume she had on the previous evening. Her hair was piled up on her head; loose strands fell either side of her face. She was so beautiful my eyes were drawn of their own accord. I'd heard the expression that such-and-such a woman's beauty took a man's breath away. That's not what happened, exactly; it was more that my lungs forgot to do their job, I don't know how long for. Eventually, by a stroke of fortune, Sid and Holly came in through the door from the kitchen area, carrying plates, and they were greeted with a commotion that jolted me into taking a great breath of air, just before I would, almost certainly, have fainted.

There were smoked salmon sandwiches made with thin slices of brown bread, with quartered lemons and black pepper. Now there was something 'to soak it up', Grandpa decided we could all have a second glass of champagne.

People rearranged themselves, and conversation resumed. Aunt Lorna was now on the big sofa opposite the fire. 'I used to play with a boys' team in Buenos Aires,' she was telling Melony. 'Every year, as I grew older, people complained. My mother said her friends in the polo club were saying things behind her back, but my father insisted that his daughters had the right to do the same as their brothers.'

It wasn't just my aunt's physical beauty. Her body possessed some kind of magnetic force; a vertiginous attraction: I was pulled towards it as if towards a cliff edge. Not that I knew what I wanted to do when I got there, other than to fall.

'If I wished to play football, he wouldn't let my mother stop me,' she said. 'I played until I was fourteen, fifteen.'

I discovered myself about to sit down on the arm of the sofa next to my aunt when Holly elbowed me in the ribs and hissed in my ear, 'Have you heard about these stupid stickers?'

'Of course I have,' I said, as if I hadn't already made it quite clear that I knew a lot more than she did about what went on in the house, owing to my summer visits, and the particular closeness of my relationship with our grandparents.

'I was there when Grandma explained it,' I said.

'It's so dumb,' Holly said. 'I mean, my Mum says she doesn't want anything to do with it, but then she told Sid she's just going to choose the bits she really loves.'

'What's wrong with that?' I asked.

'She's chosen a cracked old mirror, for one thing,' Holly said. '*And* a chamber pot! A potty, she called it.' Holly's pale cheeks flushed with anger, I couldn't really see why, but then, as if to answer me, she continued. 'Has she asked us? I mean, who's this stuff for in the end?' Holly shook her head. 'She doesn't care about us *at* all. Me and Matt and Sid are the ones who are going to end up with the rubbish she chooses.'

She saw me frowning at her and added, 'Ev*ent*ually.'

'Eventually,' I said, 'you'll pass it on as well.'

Holly grimaced, and said, 'I'm *never* having children.'

The twins were at opposite ends of the room, sat on the floor behind people's chairs, sending texts to each other: they'd peep around the side of the chair to look at each other and glance and nod towards someone else, then return to their parallel conversation, across the radio waves of the room. Otherwise the company was convivial, restrained. People spoke quietly to their neighbours. With Uncle Jonny absent there was a lack of animation to proceedings. I looked at my father, who was standing near the Christmas tree, chatting with Sid. He was holding a book – the one, I assumed, she was presently devouring – to which, in polite turn, they clearly referred. It seemed to me that the energy between the two brothers had been unequally divided; as if some of my father's due allotment had been held back, for his brother, born eighteen months later. Not that I felt, realising this, any less love for my father. It just made me feel somewhat sorry for him.

I took a plate of sandwiches around the room, offering them fleetingly to people, and managed to get back to the corner with a few left. Holly didn't want any more, neither did Xan or Baz. Smoked salmon was a developed taste, I presumed; a sign of maturity. I squeezed lemon on one, and ate it in two sumptuous mouthfuls. It was my fourth so far. In the din of chatter all around me, I wondered how many I could consume before supper.

Then, suddenly, there was a lull, of the sort that sometimes occurs in a room full of people. Each of the half-dozen conversations ceased at the same moment, except for one, to which everyone else's attention now switched: my mother was nodding, as Auntie Gwen – the two of them sat on the small sofa, over by the piano – told her, 'It's not quite twelve weeks, we're not really telling anyone yet, not even the children.' The two of them were so intent upon each other that neither noticed ten eavesdroppers surrounding them. 'Melony's been here before. Years ago. But yes.' Gwen smiled. 'We're hopeful. Really hopeful.'

My mother took hold of Gwen's hand, and it was now that, slowly, as if waking from sleep, both Mum and Auntie Gwen blinked, looked around, saw people staring at them with various expressions of puzzlement or shock.

Grandma was the first to speak. 'Are you serious?' she demanded. 'You surely cannot be serious.' She looked from Gwen across to Melony, and back to her daughter. 'Tell me it's not true.'

I was impressed, to be honest, that Grandma had cottoned on so quickly to what was going on. I only did so myself because Holly had told the twins and I the night before what her mother and mother's girlfriend were attempting, and even so I couldn't quite believe that the woman sitting next to Aunt Lorna on the big sofa had a baby growing inside her; a baby made from one of Gwen's eggs and the sperm of a chinnor male friend of theirs, mixed in a laboratory, implanted in Melony's womb; a baby who would be my cousin. Melony did, however, look different from how she had a moment before: visibly pale, stricken.

'This is outrageous,' Grandma said, standing up.

I noticed my mother catch my father's attention, and make a face as if to say both, 'Look, this is just the sort of behaviour I feared,' and 'Do something!' I glanced at Grandpa, sitting in the armchair beside the tree, Holly kneeling beside it. He was looking at Grandma unperturbed, making no attempt to intervene. Auntie Gwen began to sob. All the colour had drained from Melony's face: I'm sure if she had tried to stand up, she would have been unable to.

'Quite frankly,' Grandma said, 'I can't tell you how disappointed I am.'

It was Sid, of all people, who stepped forward. 'Look what time it is,' she said. 'The lasagne must be ready by now.' Holly scuttled out, whether hurt at discovering the news in this way or to check on the supper I wasn't sure.

'I'm not hungry,' said Grandma. She marched to the door. 'I'm going to bed.' She stopped in the doorway, turned back, and addressed the room. 'There are sixty million people on this island, do you genuinely not realise? An island capable of sustaining, what, twenty million, at most? Will you really not admit it? We've not fed ourselves for two hundred years. And *look* what they did to your father's orchards!' She looked around, her piercing eyes boring into each one of us in turn. 'Can we really expect other countries to keep supplying us with food that *they* will need? No.' She shook her head. 'No, we can't. The planet is dying, and trying desperately to save itself. Vast tracts of populated land are going to be uninhabitable. This island will be a lifeboat, an ark, that people from all over the world are going to try to cling to.'

It was the first great political speech I'd ever heard, and I heard it delivered live, in a shrill voice of barely restrained hysteria, in the drawing room of my grandparents' house in Shropshire.

'Millions of people live like the royalty of earlier epochs,' Grandma continued. 'Never have so many people lived so well. The height of civilisation, and it's built on sand. We're passing on a society in a state of decadence and you, my own children, are unable to curb your self-indulgent breeding.' My grandmother shook her vulture-like head. The head of an ailing prophet. Having given this blast, she looked suddenly frail, as if it had used up all her force. She reached out to the doorframe for support. My father leapt up from his chair and rushed over, and helped her walk towards the stairs.

Through her sobs, Auntie Gwen spoke faintly after her, 'But Melony's never had a child.'

6

Holly, the twins and I were up in the attic, each in our own alcove. Holly was sulking.

'You want to listen to some music?' Baz asked. 'You can borrow my iPod.'

'You can listen to whatever you like,' said Xan. 'Headphones. Docking station.'

Holly wouldn't be distracted. 'What is wrong with her?' she grumbled. 'She's mad. How can we even be related?'

'Fellated?' Baz asked.

'Excuse me?'

'You said, "How can we even be fellated?"'

'Don't be dizzy.'

'Didn't she say fellated?'

'No,' Xan told him.

'Why not?' Baz asked.

Dinner had been a tense, indigestive occasion. Vegetable lasagne served with carrots and Brussels sprouts. I wasn't hungry after the smoked salmon. Grandma's seat was empty, as were Auntie Gwen's and Melony's. No one had much to say until Uncle Jonny breezed in with beery breath and, though disappointed by his sister's absence, told the rest of us how Gwen's first boyfriend – now a paunchy, moustachioed father of four – had been in the pub, and had asked after her in a wistful manner.

'I thought of employing him, actually,' Uncle Jonny said, without adding what for.

'I can just imagine you outsourcing whatever it is you do out here,' my father told his brother. 'Cheap labour out in the sticks.'

'Oh, you and your *minimum* bloody wage,' Jonny said, grinning as he made his good-humoured accusation, as if Dad were the politician responsible, and not just a quiet citizen with a reasonable affection for social democracy. 'You bleeding hearts make it virtually im*possible* for entrepreneurs like us to invest in people.'

My father declined to respond to this provocation, and Jonny turned to our grandfather and said, 'In the old days, Pa, you'd have dragged us off to midnight Mass tonight.'

'Your mother and I will be attending church in the morning,' Grandpa said. 'The ten-thirty, if any of you heathens are interested.'

We ate our dessert in almost total silence. It was lemon meringue and chocolate mousse, each a speciality of our grandmother, but no one looked like they were particularly enjoying them. Afterwards, I took the dogs out for their late stretch. This time Grandpa came too. Although I knew that the dogs liked me, they cleaved to my grandfather, their master, in a quite different way: both Leda and Sel were constantly aware of him; their lives revolved around him, were spent within a limited circumference, man and dogs on one another's radar. He never beat them, according to Dad, who'd told me that there were always two setters around Grandpa – whenever possible, the children or grandchildren of their predecessors. He told me that when Grandpa was away on one of his rare business trips and telephoned home, after speaking to the children he'd ask them to excite the dogs so that, like the composer Edward Elgar had before him, he could listen to them barking.

We strolled around the riding school, the outbuildings and pile of rusting machinery, and back. Auntie Gwen's car had gone. The grey clouds of the morning had promised rain; barely a drop had fallen. I could see no moon nor a single star in the night sky, yet there was light enough to walk without stumbling. We stood on the patio, the empty stables behind us, gazing across the valley. The night was still, and silent. We could see the isolated farms strung along the far side of the valley, a necklace of orange lights.

I wanted to ask Grandpa what he was thinking about. I wanted to ask him what was going on, but I didn't know how to. After a while he let out a heavy sigh and said, 'Well, that should do them.' We went back inside and put the dogs to bed.

'I wish they had a TV up here,' Baz lamented.

'What do you like to watch?' Holly asked him.

'Sky,' he replied. 'Setanta.'

'She asked you what you watch,' Xan said.

'Plasma,' said Baz. 'HD.'

'Widescreen's okay,' Xan mused. 'And sensurround, obviously.'

'High Definition's more important,' Baz insisted.

'Of course,' Xan agreed.

It turned out, Sid came through to inform us, that Melony was too offended and upset to stay here any longer: Auntie Gwen had driven her to the railway station in Wolverhampton, where she'd caught one of the last trains back to London. Gwen had since returned to the house, and gone straight to bed.

We turned the lights out in the attic. For a while there was a strip of white beneath the door from Sid, reading in bed, but soon that too went out.

'Is your Mum going to church tomorrow?' Xan asked in the darkness.

I assumed he was addressing Holly, and she must have, too. 'No way,' she said, in a tone so neutral you couldn't tell whether Holly was loyally defending her mum from the very idea of doing something so insane, or on the other hand denying that her obtuse mother could be open to spiritual experience of any kind.

'Dad said he might go,' Baz said.

'Yes,' said Xan, 'and drag us along.'

'I'm just going to stay in bed until after they've left,' Baz decided.

'Well,' said Holly, 'since our thoughtful parents jointly agreed not to have Santa Claus deliver stockings this year, we might as well stay in bed all day.'

'She *does* believe in Father Christmas,' Baz said.

'I wish *I* did,' said Xan. 'It would be weird if our Dad's turning religious, wouldn't it?'

'It's unlikely,' Holly said.

'No, I really think he is,' said Baz.

'Maybe he's got temporal lobe damage,' Xan suggested.

'It's the only explanation. Probably a stroke.'

'He'll be turning epileptic next,' said Xan, whereupon both the twins launched into what were clearly, from the sounds they made in the darkness, the shuddering imitations of a fit.

The last thing I was going to admit was that I'd told Grandpa I'd go with him and Grandma to the service on Christmas morning. I accompanied them to church when I stayed in the summer. The truth was that I enjoyed it: the ritual was quaint and hard to make much sense of, observed by a congregation composed of a handful of people all as old as my grandparents. It was like the custom of some ancient culture, which I'd been allowed to witness before it slipped away for ever; the kind of thing Dad had once done in other countries, but I could do in our own.

It became clear after a while from the sound of their breathing that the twins – as if exhausted by their fake fits – had fallen asleep. I wasn't too bothered by the prospect of their inevitable disdain of my church attendance, but I was more heedful of Holly's opinion. Just then she switched the light on inside her alcove, leaned out and said to me, 'You know what I think, Theo? You know how people say, like, an artist sometimes feels like God? First there was a God, who created everything. An artist might get a sense of this creative power in herself.'

It seemed that Holly didn't just draw pictures; she also thought about why she did so.

'I reckon,' she said, 'like, the opposite is true: people drew pictures on the walls of their caves. And these people – these artists – thought, "Perhaps there is a mind behind our minds. Creating us, just as we create these images."'

I didn't say anything. I was stunned, actually. Amazed. It was the first time I'd met someone who seemed to think like me. I mean, my parents did a bit, I supposed, but both of them were more interested in how people interacted with each other than what went on inside their minds.

'You mean artists gave other people the idea of God?'
Holly nodded.

'You could well be right,' I told her. I recall now how exciting this conversation was: my cousin was the first person I felt I could share my own ideas with; ideas that till then were kept in a sealed part of my brain. 'You know what I think, Hol?' I said. 'I think we have a hidden spirit, a kind of guardian. Every one of us. We're not really aware of it. Its influence is subtle. It works somehow without us knowing. What it's doing is helping us to our destiny, sort of, I don't know, steering us towards challenges we need, developing the talents we have.'

'But it's secret,' Holly said. 'I like that.'

'Yes,' I said, 'and what's really amazing is that this guardian is actually the permanent bit of us, which continues from one life to the next.'

Holly looked at me in a way that, I felt sure, mirrored the way I'd looked at her.

'You mean reincarnation?' she asked. I nodded. She smiled. 'You mean like there's no such thing as death?'

I shook my head. 'I don't think so,' I said.

III

I

Grandpa had replenished the birdfeeders by the time I got up, and was down in the near pasture, the dogs scampering around him, racing after their noses, chasing scents left by animals in the night. The tits flocked and mobbed hungrily, joined by house sparrows and a greenfinch.

Grandma was not beside the Aga. My father, Uncle Jonny and Auntie Gwen were, however, over at the table, heads bent towards each other.

'You've spoken to her already this morning?' Dad asked. 'Is she okay?'

'An apology would help,' Gwen told him.

When he caught sight of me, Dad said, 'Be a good fellow, Theo, and take Mum a cup of tea.'

I did as I was asked, and carried a mug of strong tea out of the kitchen and back upstairs. A house whose rooms are occupied by people sleeping feels, as you walk along its corridors, curiously alive – in a way that it doesn't when everyone's up and about. A stair tread squeaked beneath my foot; a floorboard creaked. I didn't wish to wake anyone. I understood why my father never wanted to lose this place; he wanted his parents to be here for ever, the house ever ready to return to. My dear, impractical papa.

The room was pitch black. I felt my way to Mum's bedside table and she let out a tired groan of thanks.

When I returned downstairs, Grandpa was back inside,

making a pot of coffee. The aroma of the ground beans when he opened the tin was delicious; it was hard to believe that he was about to make such a bitter, disgusting drink with them. 'I just saw it,' he told me. 'It's paid us a visit on Christmas Day.'

Uncle Jonny was gathering knives and spoons from the cutlery drawer. 'Who has?' he asked.

'No one you know,' Grandpa told him. 'A feathered friend of Theo's and mine.'

Jonny made no response. I didn't think he even listened to the end of the sentence, was already making his way back to the table.

'Keep your eyes peeled,' Grandpa quietly advised me. 'He may be back.'

'Do you think so?' I whispered, as heartened at this prospect as by Grandpa's choosing me to confide in.

Grandpa took the jug of coffee to the table. The others were all sat at his end, Jonny with his back to the kitchen, facing Dad – next to Grandpa – and Auntie Gwen. I sat quietly along from my aunt, and bowed my head over a bowl of cereal.

'Happy Christmas, my children,' Grandpa said. 'Thank you again for coming.'

We ate fresh bread with the home-made jams, drank tea or coffee or juice. Aunt Lorna entered the kitchen, dressed in her running outfit; as she did so my attention was taken out of my control, helpless as the needle of a compass, and turned towards her. She came around the side of the island and stood across the table from me, half-turned towards the others.

'Another tranquil day,' she said, looking through the wide set of windows behind Gwen, Dad and myself.

'Quite still,' Grandpa agreed.

'It's like being on the deck of a ship here, isn't it?' Lorna said. 'Becalmed on a green ocean.'

'Have you been out?' Gwen asked.

'I'm just off,' Lorna said. She stood there in her skintight gear, pinning her hair up behind her head, a hairgrip between her teeth. 'Ideal for running,' she said, taking the grip from her mouth.

I had the sudden notion that I was the last surviving member of an old family, the remnants of the previous generations also sitting at this table, while Aunt Lorna belonged to a superior tribe of beautiful athletes, who never grew older. She knew this. She wanted us to know it. That's what she was doing, somehow, as she stood there, pinning her hair up: asserting a subtle distance from the family she'd married into, improved, taken in a different direction. She gazed outside, across towards the coach house and outbuildings, and said, 'I think I'll run that way today.'

I glanced at the others. Grandpa was looking at his daughter-in-law. So were Auntie Gwen and my father. I didn't know whether they had similar thoughts to my own. Only Uncle Jonny, the man who had snared Lorna, with whom she'd had children, ignored her, and munched toast.

'See you later,' Aunt Lorna said, and left.

None of the others said anything for a moment or two, until Uncle Jonny swallowed the last mouthful of tea from his cup and said, 'Not like Ma to stay in bed.'

'She's tired,' Grandpa told him.

Again there was a pause, then my father said, 'I'm trying to remember when Ma started railing at the imminent collapse of civilisation.'

'The coming apocalypse,' said Uncle Jonny. 'But it's becoming obsessive, isn't it?'

'Well, you can hardly say that she's wrong, can you?' Dad said.

'Still,' said Auntie Gwen, 'there's no excuse for attacking people the way she did.'

There was another pause. It was as if the things they were saying stirred up dust around them, and they needed to wait a moment for the dust to settle before moving on.

'Yes,' said Uncle Jonny. 'You have to admit, Pa. Ma's never bothered to bite her tongue.' He laughed, and the laugh contained a lifetime's memories of rudeness, insults, outbursts. 'But she seems, I don't know. There's a fury to it that's new.'

I noticed that Grandpa had been staring at his plate for some while. He wasn't the kind of man to lose his temper. But his stillness, I realised, was not calm but the containment of emotion. The others seemed to realise this as well: their attention turned towards him. He spoke quietly, slowly. 'Is it not obvious?' he said. 'Have you really no idea?'

As soon as he said it, everything changed. Instantly, it was clear, they had a very good idea.

'Oh, no,' said Auntie Gwen. My father put his hand out, and held hers. 'Oh, Pa,' she said.

'What?' Uncle Jonny demanded. He looked from Gwen to Grandpa, and then at Dad. 'What?'

My father didn't say anything. He held his sister's hand, slowly shook his head.

'She's dying,' Grandpa said, the words barely escaping the anger contained by his lips.

After another long pause, Dad asked, 'How?'

'Brain tumour,' Grandpa said.

'Does she know?' Dad asked.

'Of course she bloody knows,' Grandpa said. 'She's dealing with it with the same bloody-mindedness and courage she's dealt with everything else in her life.'

I sat there, a mute witness. I didn't feel anything. Auntie Gwen managed to speak through her sobs. 'Can nothing be done?'

Grandpa sighed. 'It's deep inside her skull,' he said. 'They can't get to it, you see.'

'Is Ma in pain?' Uncle Jonny asked.

'A constant headache,' Grandpa said. 'Most afternoons I hear her vomiting in our bathroom. She's barely taken in any sustenance for weeks now. She has visual disturbances. Driving's out of the question.'

Uncle Jonny put his elbows on the table and his head in his hands. 'Oh, God,' he said.

'I trust the three of you appreciate she'd be furious if she found out that I'd told you,' Grandpa said. Then, as if noticing me there for the first time, he said, 'I'm so sorry, Theo.'

'What are your plans, Pa?' my father asked.

Uncle Jonny sat up straight. 'Plans?' he spat. 'What kind of ridiculous bloody question is that?'

Grandpa ignored him. 'The hospice in Shrewsbury is excellent,' he said, his grey eyes filling with tears. He took a deep breath, sniffed, and said, 'It's the circulation of cerebro-spinal fluid, you see, it's obstructed by the tumour.' Dad put his right hand on Grandpa's left hand, on the table. 'That's what's causing the impairment of her mental functioning. Sending her off on these rants. They're giving her drugs, corticosteroids, to reduce the swelling. But the drugs seem to make her even sicker.'

Dad shook his head. Gwen leaned against his shoulder, weeping. Uncle Jonny buried his head back in his hands. Grandpa gazed at nothing, his head bowed. The numbness inside me was, I could tell, beginning to thaw. Like the feeling you get when you know you're going to be sick, not exactly now this instant but at some moment in the extremely near and inevitable future, I could sense a distant wave, not of nausea but of sadness. I shifted my attention to the collection of conserves on the marble carousel in the middle of the table: *blackberry and apple jam, Aug 2006*; *greengage jelly, 2007*; *raspberry jam, Jul 2007*; *strawberry jam, 2007*. It struck me that none of them were from this year, and I knew that if I were to look in the larder there'd be none there. Grandma hadn't made any this year. We were already living on her reserve supplies, just as she was.

Grandpa took a deep breath, as if he needed it for buoyancy, and raised himself up. 'We'll be leaving for church at ten, if anyone wants to join us.'

I waited till Grandpa had left the room and then, before anyone could say anything to me, I got up and ran outside.

2

My grandparents' house, built in its own grounds on the slope of Brown Clee Hill, lay on a parish boundary. The large village, with the pub that Uncle Jonny had visited the night before, a garage, a butcher and a baker, and a post office and stores where my grandmother did her shopping – it was virtually a small town – lay to the east. For some reason, however, my grandparents attended the tiny church in the scattered hamlet to the west. Grandma had had an argument with the churchwarden or organist or somebody years before, and she'd refused to set foot in the large village church ever since. Or perhaps it had even been her father? I couldn't quite recall. Some obstinate vendetta.

I was the only other member of the family to travel the short journey with them that Christmas morning. My mother approved of my choice. 'It's good for children to be bored,' she reckoned. 'It stimulates the imagination.'

My grandfather's car, though almost new, already smelled of dogs, and was cramped. I sat in the middle of the back seat with my legs folded, leaning forward. Leda and Sel had opted to come along, too, though they'd have to remain in the car; they sat on the floor of the vehicle, one on either side of me.

'Let's hope it's not that awful man,' Grandma said in the passenger seat.

'Could be any one of them,' Grandpa said, driving slowly. 'From any of the Corvedale churches.'

The congregation consisted of no more than a dozen members, dispersed around the pews of the small church. I was the youngest by about sixty years. Seven electric bar heaters hung from the roof beams, their orange glowing filaments sending a meagre heat further up into the rafters. There was a pervasive smell of damp stone; of old wood and musty books, warming slowly.

A Christmas tree stood in the corner up by the altar. The hymn board, with numerals slotted in, had tinsel around it. Fairy lights twinkled along the top of the screen, in front of which was a nativity scene in a wooden stable peopled by squat, home-made figures – of Mary and Joseph and the baby Jesus, shepherds, the three wise men – so ugly they were practically blasphemous.

We sat in pensive silence. On the wall above my head an ancient electric meter made a noise like a dog panting. Below me, attached to hooks beneath the shelf on which we'd placed our hymn books and order of service sheets, hung kneelers embroidered, Grandpa told me, by parishioners: each person had depicted the house they lived in. He pointed out that the endeavour was a kind of subversive parable: regardless of what sort of dwellings they were, from his own virtual manor to the meanest cottage, on the kneelers they'd been rendered all the same size.

The priest stumbled in, tall, thin and stooping, old as his congregation, flustered. 'Just come from Clee St Margaret,' he apologised, breathless, as if he'd run over the hills. 'The nine-thirty.' He rushed up to the chancel, and within moments launched into the communion service.

* * *

Before long an even older man staggered along the nave to the lectern, holding on to the ends of the pews as he went, to give a reading from the Epistle of Paul to Titus. It was all about how Titus was left in Crete and told to ordain elders in every city there. 'A bishop must be blameless,' the man read in a faltering voice. 'Not given to wine, no striker, not given to filthy lucre.' It was an odd piece of scripture, which grew increasingly mad as he read on. 'There are many unruly and vain talkers and deceivers, specially they of the circumcision, whose mouths must be stopped, who subvert whole houses, teaching things which they ought not, for filthy lucre's sake.'

I stole a glance around the scattered members of the congregation. Each appeared to have his or her mind on other things; on other Christmases perhaps, long past. The words being read out washed over them, unheard. I hoped Grandpa had a copy of the Bible in his library: I looked forward to finding this passage and reading it to Holly. 'One of themselves, even a prophet of their own, said, The Cretans are always liars, evil beasts, slow bellies. This witness is true. Wherefore rebuke them sharply, that they may be sound in the faith.'

I went up to the altar rail along with everyone else to take the Eucharist, even though I'd not been confirmed. The priest didn't realise. The thin wafer sat on my tongue; the wine was a shock of alcohol in the morning. I savoured it, and swallowed the bread walking back to our pew, feeling older than my years. There were prayers: I knelt, squeezed shut my eyes and begged God to make my grandmother well, and keep her well for ever. It seemed unlikely that a God I had no conception of would answer my plea, but perhaps this was itself one of those challenges of faith religion was famous for.

During the hymns, while the congregation made a pitiful

collective attempt at both melody and volume, I stared down at my hymn book: my voice was even more unpredictable when asked to sing as when speaking, and so I kept dumb. The small upright organ was located in the chancel, where we could all see it, the organist a tiny, birdlike woman perched on a stool, who played with great gusto and sang along tunelessly but loudly, giving some life to the hymns, which might otherwise have expired on the wing.

After the end of the service, while my grandparents conversed with their fellow celebrants, I studied wall tablets. On one was written, *This tablet is erected by public subscription to the sacred memory of the soldiers from this parish who fell in action in the Great War*. It was dated 1914–1919, which I knew from our study of Wilfred Owen's poems the previous term to be erroneous: the First World War ended in 1918. Perhaps this remote place existed at a slight angle to, dislocated from, the main current of events.

Outside the sky was changing, the cloud cover breaking up. There were patches of blue and white. The priest hurried away, and the other members of the congregation limped to their cars. Grandma went over to her family tomb – of course, I remembered, that was the chief reason she came to this church.

'We'll leave her be,' Grandpa said, so we kept apart. 'She'll be buried here,' he told me. 'With her parents; her older brother, who died in Burma; and her sister, who was only a child.'

I wasn't sure I understood. 'What about you, Grandpa?' I asked. 'Won't you two be side by side?'

He smiled. 'I expect so, old son. Come over here. I don't think I've ever shown you this.'

We walked across the churchyard, between graves, and stood by the fence looking out across a large, sloping field.

'What do you see?' my grandfather asked me.

The field looked, at first, just like any other parcel of rolling pasture. But as I studied it I began to perceive that the surface was variegated, with subtle hillocks, with dips and mounds. It was as if they became visible, were brought forth, only by our attention.

'There was something else here,' I tentatively suggested. It was more of a question than a statement.

Grandpa nodded. 'This was the site of the original village, until it was struck by the Black Death, the plague, in the fourteenth century. By thirteen fifty it was deserted.' He spoke of this time as if he remembered it. 'Gypsies moved in,' he continued. 'Camped here. There's been Gypsy blood in the village ever since.' Grandpa chuckled. 'I tell your grand-mother it explains the sallow skin and the brown eyes of her family.'

'Is that true?' I asked, thrilled at the prospect of Gypsy blood reeling through my veins.

'I've been teasing her with it all her life,' he answered. 'I can just about get away with it, Theo, but I wouldn't recommend that you start. Whether it's true or not, who can say? For an island race, we're wonderfully mongrel.'

We rejoined Grandma, who took my left arm as we walked slowly out of the churchyard. Squeezing her bony arm with my right hand, I imagined a time a year from now, next year's Christmas morning; imagined her not walking along this path but there, in her family tomb. All I could think of was how little I knew: of truth, of God, of those people I knew best. People are put in the ground, I thought, like buried books, the stories they've acted out buried with them. What remained above? Faint, fading rumours?

I would in time inherit my grandfather's library. It held two thousand, seven hundred and twenty-three volumes, including pamphlets and maps, and a pocket edition of A. E. Housman's *A Shropshire Lad* that he used to keep in the glove compartment of his car. My parents kindly stored it for me until the time came when I was able to buy my own house, whereupon the first thing I did was to put shelves up around the walls of the small rooms, using cheap L-shaped brackets, and floorboards rescued from skips. I hired a van and transported the books in large cardboard boxes from Oxford.

I've hung on to the library ever since, through half a dozen moves, into marriage and a family of my own. Although actually that's not strictly true: over the years I've probably given away – to charity shops, mostly – about half the books I inherited; but only when I had new ones of my own to replace them with, including many of my own parents' books, when their time came. The size of the library has, until recently, remained very much the same as it was.

I'm not entirely sure of the reason for this. It can't be explained merely by the exigencies of space: the house we've ended up in is twice the size of my first and could accommodate a greater number of books. I've come to the conclusion that, as an adolescent, I conceived the notion of my grandfather as a civilised man, and, further, that his library expressed this, was appropriate for such a man and his family, available to its members to browse, delve into, borrow from as they will. The prospect of accumulating more and more books felt profligate, intellectually gluttonous. I suspect, too, I would have felt burdened by the weight of obsolete knowledge, superceded by new research. The process of winnowing, on the other hand, deciding which books to remove to make way for an influx of fresh ones, invigorating for the health of the stock, is an essential task of any librarian, as necessary as the regular culling of a herd of deer.

3

Upon returning to the house I searched for my parents and found them, to my surprise, in my grandparents' bedroom. They were speaking to each other in hushed voices. 'I've always rather coveted Pa's chest of drawers,' my father said. In his left hand he held a sheet of blue stickers.

They each gave a little start when they realised they'd been interrupted. Relieved to discover that it was me, they resumed their investigations. 'It's very dark wood,' said my mother, frowning. 'Nineteenth century, like most everything else. Mahogany, I should think. And look: it hasn't got legs. I wouldn't be surprised if it was the upper part of something else, like a . . . you know, what are those things called?'

'A tallboy?' Dad wondered. 'Maybe. I seem to remember being told it was Scottish.'

'I prefer that wardrobe over there,' said Mum. 'Don't you?'

My cousins were in the drawing room. The twins wanted to sort the presents into piles according to the recipient, in preparation for opening them that afternoon, but Holly was making them wait until she'd taken a photo or two, using her camera as a kind of sketchbook.

'I hate digital,' Xan told her.

'The trouble is it's fake,' Baz agreed.

'I like the grain of thirty-five mill,' said Xan. He was staring hard at a cuboid shape wrapped in thin Christmas paper that had his name on it, trying to make out the object within.

'We've got a processing lab at school,' Baz explained.

'I love photography,' Xan said.

'Who do you like?' Sidney, on the sofa, asked from behind her book.

'Kodak,' Xan replied.

'Agfa's better,' Baz said.

'Fuji used to be good,' Xan said. 'But their green's not the same as it was.'

'Cibachrome's the best,' Baz decided.

'That's very true,' Xan solemnly agreed.

Uncle Jonny was outside the French windows, talking on his mobile. It seemed extraordinary to be conducting business on Christmas Day, but it was clear that he was, from the way he was standing, feet planted on the ground two feet apart. I went out, as he concluded his call.

'The fuckers were desperate to buy a month ago,' he said. 'Now I want to sell they're not interested? You tell them no one kicks me in the bollocks and walks away.' He snapped shut what I thought of as his profanity phone, put it back in the left-hand back pocket of his jeans. The day was colder than yesterday, though it didn't seem so, since wide swathes of the sky were now blue. Uncle Jonny wore a pink, open-necked shirt, with gold cufflinks. He turned and found me standing there, like some shivering acolyte. 'Let me give you a word of advice, Theo,' he said. 'When your business is doing well, borrow as much money as you can. You know why?'

I considered the question carefully, though I hardly knew whether it was the kind of puzzle to be answered with common sense and logic. 'You can make the business bigger?' I ventured.

Jonny shook his head. 'Number one,' he said, 'you pay yourself a dividend out of that money. Number two, it's good to have debt whose interest you're obliged to service. You know why?'

Sensing I was unlikely to know the correct answer to this one either I shook my head.

'Because,' Jonny said, 'it motivates you and the people who work for you to perform better.' He grinned. 'I'll tell you a secret, Theo. It's all about confidence. Of course. Everyone knows that. People look at me and say, "We'll trust him with our money, he's such a confident bastard." I know that. But that's not what drives me; not confidence. Fear. That's what drives us. Fear of failure. Shame. Ruin.'

Having delivered himself of this counsel, Uncle Jonny looked around him, as if for a better audience, then up at the walls and eaves of the house. 'Funny old place, this, eh?' he said.

I mumbled agreement. 'Have you finished putting your stickers on the furniture yet?' I asked, anxious that I was being presumptuous in doing so.

'Me?' my uncle replied. His grimace suggested I'd accused him of indecent exposure. 'Not my area, antiques,' he said, shaking his head. 'Women's business. I've left all that sticker stuff to Lorna.'

'But what about furniture in your own room?' I asked. 'From your childhood?'

Uncle Jonny shook his head. 'They mean nothing to me. Bits of junk.' He gave a sudden tremble of his wide, solid shoulders. 'Love and power, Theo,' he said. 'That's all that counts. It's bloody cold out here. You coming in?'

Grandma had agreed to let others cook the main meal later, but she'd insisted on preparing a light lunch of pumpkin soup with home-made rolls, along with the ham, Stilton, cheddar. Finding her on her own in the kitchen, I told her all about the stickers: that Auntie Gwen was choosing furniture based on sentiment for her childhood, Lorna was selecting the finest antiques, and my Mum and Dad were doing both of these, while also trying to second-guess what the others were doing. I was aware of my filial disloyalty, but the fact was it distressed me to find them assessing Grandma's furniture the very day they'd learned that she was mortally ill. I hardly appreciated that they might be holding their sorrow at arm's length, in whatever way they could; that it would come back for us all after dark.

My account filled Grandma with glee. It may have been that I exaggerated a little as I went along.

'Look at them,' she said. 'Like hyenas, snarling over the bones of an old carcass.' She cackled with delight. 'I've let the dogs loose, you see.'

The only trouble was that, possessed of a febrile energy, Grandma moved quickly between the kitchen, the pantry and the larder – with its deep freeze and an extra fridge – so that I couldn't just whisper, but had to follow her around in order to keep up the conversation, and although I spoke as quietly as I could she kept saying, 'Speak up, boy!' and 'Don't swallow your words!' I was certain people could hear.

'My advice, Theo,' Grandma said, 'is don't have them yourself.'

'Have what?' I asked.

'Children, of course. Awful things. Dreadful.' She screwed

up her wrinkled face as she reached for a jar of chutney.
'Horrid.'

'Why did *you*?' I asked her.

'Oh, one did in those days. One didn't imagine one had a choice, you see.' She carried a tureen back to the kitchen. 'One was an ignorant little bitch, really. Where's Holly? Would you two go and get me some apples. You know where they're stored, don't you?'

The apple loft was above Grandpa's workshop. We climbed the wooden staircase, dimly lit by a small window greyed by dust and cobwebs, and came out in a room whose smell was over-powering: sweet, musty, decaying and delicious all at once, in one complexity of scent that I inhaled deeply, my nostrils greedy for it.

I wasn't sure Holly even noticed the smell. It was the sight that captivated her: apples laid out on wooden trays, in specially constructed racks. She slid trays out, revealing all sorts of size, shape, shade of colour. Each variety was identified by marker pen on a white plastic tab tacked to its tray: Ribston Pippin, Catshead, Ashmead's Kernel.

'I'm coming back here this afternoon to start a still-life,' Holly said, and it was true that it was as if we'd stepped inside an old painting. 'I'm not even going to take any photos.'

'The apples are breathing, you know,' I told her. 'They inhale oxygen just like us, exhale carbon dioxide. To store them through the winter the air has to be monitored, and changed when necessary. It's called gas storage.'

We picked some of the odder-looking specimens from assorted trays, and put them in the basket we'd brought with us. Holly was looking around the store, nodding at the trays, her lips moving: she was clearly making calculations.

'I don't quite get it,' she said. 'There must be a thousand apples in here – I mean, I've never seen so many in one place – but I can't see how Grandpa could have made all his money just from these. Are they really rare and expensive, or what?'

I didn't mean to laugh. I tried to swallow my derision as soon as it leapt from my mouth, but too late. In the murky room I saw Holly's brown eyes narrow. How was it, I wondered, that our grandfather's laughter lacked cruelty or scorn, and was not hurtful? Why couldn't mine be the same?

'These are just from the little orchard over there,' I said, pointing through the wall. 'Next to the drive. The most sheltered spot here, apparently. Grandpa planted his favourite varieties after he retired. The business was down south, he had hundreds of acres, in Herefordshire mostly. The standard lay-out was a hundred and thirty-four trees to an acre. Thousands of tons of apples a year, boxes driven on lorries all around the country every week.'

'Where to?'

'Markets, I suppose,' I conjectured. 'Shops. Supermarkets.'

We climbed back down the stairs. 'What happened to the business, anyway?' Holly asked. 'Why didn't your dad or my mum or Uncle Jonny take it over?'

I shrugged. 'I'm not sure,' I admitted. 'But Grandpa said the whole industry died on its feet. We eat apples sent in refrigerated ships from all over the world now. South Africa. America. New Zealand.'

Holly and I crossed the yard. Behind us, my father and Aunt Lorna were having a stroll in the riding school, the dogs stretching their legs around them. 'What are they doing?' Holly asked.

'As long as they're not planning another football match,' I said.

On the way back into the house we were ambushed in the hallway by the twins, who leapt out from beneath the stairs like a pair of trolls.

'Where have you two been?' Xan demanded.

We showed him the fruit we'd collected.

Baz was staring at us. 'I know what you two have been up to,' he said in a sinister tone of voice.

'Urgh,' said Xan. 'Yes, you're right.'

'Kissing cousins,' said Baz.

Holly pushed past them with the basket, and made for the kitchen, but I had a failure of nerve and stood where I was, loath to validate their insinuations.

'That's incest,' said Xan.

'It's sick,' Baz agreed.

'Don't be ridiculous,' I stuttered.

'He's gone red,' said Xan.

'No, I haven't,' I said, feeling my cheeks suffuse with heat.

'Why are you blushing, Theo?' Baz wondered, all innocence.

I was saved by our grandfather, coming up from his study into the hallway. 'Where's Rosemary?' he said. 'I've got an email from Matt. Happy Christmas to everyone, especially his grandmother. Still stuck in Bristol, poor fellow. Seems he has a final English essay to finish off now. Joining us tomorrow.'

4

We ate lunch in a hurry, but by the time everything had been cleared away, the dishwasher stacked and switched on, then preparations for the main meal made – potatoes peeled, cabbage cut, the stalks of a hundred sprouts nicked – and we'd cajoled and herded everyone into the drawing room, it was two p.m.: we only had an hour before the Queen's speech, and I was as anxious as the twins to open all our presents. I needn't have worried. Xan and Baz piled each person's gifts in front of them and, following a mealtime etiquette, as soon as Grandma picked up one of hers so we were all free to unwrap our own. Ten minutes later all of my generation – and two or three of our parents' – had ripped open their Christmas presents in a communal frenzy. No sooner had each of us identified a gift, and hurled the wrapping paper into a pile in the middle of the room, than we grabbed the next, pausing only to say a fleeting thank you to whoever in the room had bestowed it. We took neither pleasure nor interest in any item but laid it aside at once and seized upon the next like crows who, Grandpa told me, do not consume whole fruit but peck a bite from one cherry or raspberry and move on to another, creating havoc with their greed.

The refuse of scrunched-up wrapping paper filled the middle of the large room. Those who resisted this mass hysteria could only watch from the side and complain in plaintive tones. 'But I want to see what everyone else has got,' my mother lamented, while Aunt Lorna said, 'Xan, please, I'm trying to make a list. Baz, who gave you that iPod Touch?'

Afterwards we went back through our new possessions and tried to identify who they were from. My cousins had given me a camera.

'Sorry it's digital,' said Xan. 'Mum got it.'

'It is eighteen megapixels,' his brother pointed out. 'With a telephoto lens.'

'We thought you might like to be a paparazzi,' Xan told me.

'Paparazzo,' his brother corrected. 'Yes, you've got that sort of lurking quality, Theo.'

'Shifty,' said Xan.

'Just the type to take embarrassing photos of celebs.'

'For magazines,' Xan agreed. 'Coming out of the gym.'

'Underarm bristle.'

'Damp crotches.'

'The shots the stars don't want us to see.'

'*Heat*,' Xan said.

'*Nuts*,' said Baz.

My grandfather gave me a secondhand book: *The Stories of the Greeks*. 'Tracked it down on the Internet,' Grandpa told me. Greek myths, from Ovid, Homer, Virgil and the plays of Euripides, retold by Rex Warner. This book would turn out to be, in actual fact, the single volume that got me reading, in the car on the way home, two days later (when I would discover that reading while being driven no longer made me sick). The creation, or recreation, of an inner world, intense and vivid as the real one, prompted by small symbolic marks on paper. This miracle. I've read that book many times; more than once each decade since.

'Christmas is a time for celebration,' the Queen began her speech. 'But this year it is a more sombre occasion for many.'

'Very true,' Auntie Gwen agreed.

Holly and Sid were boycotting the broadcast, as were my parents, who were both ardent republicans, although Dad professed a soft spot for the future king, Prince Charles, whose inappropriately expressed opinions – about architecture, farming, education – my father tended to agree with.

'Those who have seemed to me,' the Queen said, 'to be the most happy, contented and fulfilled have always been the people who have lived the most outgoing and unselfish lives, the kind of people who are generous with their talents or their time.'

'Hear, hear,' said Grandma. Uncle Jonny, beside her, turned to his sons, and nodded agreement.

We were invited to dress up for dinner. After some nagging from my mother I consented to iron my best T-shirt and jeans. We set up the ironing board in their bedroom. Mum was in the bathroom along the corridor. Dad had a fancy shirt with ruffs down the front, which I ironed for him. He put it on and then spent ages trying to push a cufflink through each set of sleeves one-handed, instead of doing so with two hands before he put the shirt on, an act of basic incompetence typical of my father.

There was a knock at the door and Auntie Gwen came in. 'There you are,' she said, and sat on Mum's bed, facing her brother.

'Are you okay?' Dad asked, in a voice that suggested she'd not been earlier, and it occurred to me that I may have been unfair on them: while I'd been to church with my grandparents perhaps everyone else had been at home sharing the news of our grandmother's illness with my cousins; explaining her prognosis.

'I wish they weren't such a long way from London,' Gwen said, which seemed to me an odd way of putting what she wanted to say. It was she, and her brothers, who'd travelled away from the Marches. But I said nothing, only sprayed some water from the iron on to my T-shirt.

'We'll all be coming to and fro,' Dad said, as he pressed the stud laboriously through a sleeve.

'Let me help with that,' Gwen said, and she reached forward and took over. 'Do you know what Lorna told me just now?' She said they'd got next term's school fees covered, but she had no idea about the future.'

'What on earth is she talking about?' Dad said. 'Their house alone must be worth millions.'

'I don't know,' Gwen shrugged. 'That's what she said. You realise, of course, he has plans for this place?'

'Jonny?' Dad said. As Auntie Gwen threaded his cufflinks so they leaned closer together. I could barely make out what they said. 'We can fight that battle when the time comes. Who knows what the landscape will be then? Just so long as he leaves it alone while Pa's around.'

'I'm not sure. I get the feeling Pa's contemplating moving out.'

'What do you mean? Don't be silly, Gwen. Neither Ma nor Pa would ever leave here, not of their own accord.'

'There you go,' Gwen said, patting Dad's wrist. He thanked her. 'That's a very nice shirt,' she said. 'Rather chic for my big brother.'

'One has to splash out now and then,' he replied, shrugging.

'Where's it from?' Gwen asked.

'Animal Sanctuary Shop in Summertown,' Dad said, gratified his sister had taken the bait. 'Two pounds fifty. Well, you know how it is: the family clothing budget goes on Theo's gear. Costs a fortune to look that scruffy.'

I ignored them, pretending to concentrate on the ironing.

'How's Melony?' Dad asked. 'You've been in touch?'

Auntie Gwen nodded. 'We spoke just now.'

'Have you told her about Ma?'

'Yes.' Gwen shook her head. Her ringlets shivered. 'I shouldn't have. She was angry before. Now I've made her feel guilty as well. I mean, I tried to tell her Ma could be just as snippy and imperious before she was ill, but it's hard to believe if you don't know her.'

'Amy would have gladly taken the train, too,' Dad said, smiling.

It was my turn to bang the gong, six times, for Christmas dinner. Each peal resounded through the house and seemed to die in corridors, in empty rooms, but presently people came forth, in their finery, and we gathered at the dining-room table. Holly and Sid had set it with our grandmother's fancy willow-pattern china. The only lighting was from candles, set on the table and the window sills.

Aunt Lorna wore the most elegant black dress I'd ever seen. I suspected it must have been made especially for her by some designer, who wanted us to see her bare, olive-skinned shoulders and arms, and to not see but somehow imagine we knew even better the gorgeous rest of her. It was some sort of magic of tailoring, I supposed. I felt the urge to reach over and hug my aunt, but Sidney, after helping her Mum serve everyone at the island, flopped her skinny self down between us.

To my right, Holly sat next to me. She wore a tight red top and another short skirt, this time with tights like a Harlequin's, different coloured diamond patterns shaped to her legs. She and Sid were also wearing make-up for the first time that I'd seen; Holly's cross-eyes seemed a little wider; her lips shone.

Grandpa and Uncle Jonny wore dinner jackets with bow ties, as did the twins; they looked like they were attending a film premiere in Leicester Square. But as soon as we opened the crackers and put on our crêpe crowns, the effect was spoiled, and the men all looked like drunken buffoons. The women fared better, somehow; though not a great deal.

We ate turkey with rolled bacon, roast potatoes, parsnips, sweet potatoes, green cabbage and Brussels sprouts, and a delicious stuffing everyone congratulated Grandma on. 'The pièce de résistance, Ma,' cried Uncle Jonny. There was nut roast for the London vegetarians from south of the river, made by Auntie Gwen, but Melony had gone and Holly seemed to have become a part-time carnivore, which left Gwen and Sid eating it on their own.

'What do you call a rhino with a funny face?' Uncle Jonny read. He'd bought the crackers at Harrods, but the jokes were just as bad as cheap ones. 'Sir.'

Gwen sat next to Grandpa, where Melony had been. Our grandfather told us the story of an old family holiday. 'It might have been the last one we all took together. We stayed in that villa on the hill up above Menton, remember?'

'Rod wanted to play ping-pong the whole time,' said Uncle Jonny. 'Nagged us all, one after the other.'

'It was worth it,' Dad said, with a modest shrug. 'Without

those hours of altitude training I might never have achieved an international ranking.'

'Owned by that crazy Russian woman,' Auntie Gwen recalled. 'The Countess.'

'We were invaded by huge ants,' Gwen laughed.

'Ma dealt with them,' my father said. 'She found a blowtorch in the basement.'

Grandma sat at the end of the table, an unreal smile on her thin lips, looking bemused. Auntie Gwen looked more relaxed than she had since we'd arrived. She'd wept, and she'd drunk some fine wine, but it was also clear that there was less tension for her without her partner here. It would have been easier for Dad, too, if Mum had gone home earlier, or even not come at all; perhaps for Uncle Jonny, as well; Aunt Lorna's presence inhibited him to some extent. Without their partners these siblings, our parents, could have reverted more easily to the way they were. The in-laws were the interlopers. The rest of us were blood: there were connections between us, whether we liked it or not.

'Anyhow,' Grandpa said, and, as each of us finished our main course, placing knife and fork on the plate, we settled down to listen to him. 'What I remember most vividly from that holiday is how Gwen here, who couldn't have been any older than you two,' – he nodded towards Holly and myself – 'took to swimming.'

'Oh, yes,' Dad said. 'That's right, Pa.'

'I suppose she must have been a decent swimmer, but I wasn't aware of it. We got to the French coast and Gwen simply,' – Grandpa raised his right hand, and watched it float off into the air away from him – 'swam out to sea. Further, and further, until she was no more than a speck, disappearing. Your mother and I tried to hide our anxiety; from each other, as we discovered afterwards, as well as from the rest of you.' We glanced at Grandma, as she was included in the reminiscence, but she appeared to have no recollection, only gazed blankly in Grandpa's direction. 'We conspired to ignore Gwen's disappearance,' he continued. 'But I'd keep looking out to sea, and not be able to spot her. Sometimes I couldn't help myself from asking one of you boys whether you could make out her tiny head, bobbing way out there in the deep distance. And you always could. My own middle-aged eyesight deteriorating. Gwen did this long-distance swim every day of the holiday. Each time my little girl swam a bit further out, was gone from my sight that little bit longer.'

The room was silent in the candlelight. All of our attention was on Grandpa, who paused at this point. Auntie Gwen put a hand on his, and he looked at her and smiled, and then around at the rest of us.

'When she reappeared it was like a miracle. She swam slowly back towards land, coming gradually closer, until she rose out of the sea, and walked towards us through the shallows, the water lapping around her ankles, a different person than she had been. Not a stranger, I don't mean. A child no longer. A young woman now, I suppose.'

Dessert was another of Grandma's specialities: chocolate roulade with fruit as well as cream inside the rolled log; along with Christmas pudding and brandy butter.

'Your grandmother made Christmas pudding last week, boys,' Uncle Jonny told the twins. 'But not this one. This one she made the week before Christmas *last* year. The one made last week is in the larder for *next* year.'

I didn't know whether everyone else realised the implications of what Jonny had said, but some of us surely did. My mother came over from the Aga with a pan and poured hot brandy over the pudding, which my father ignited with a lighter from his pocket, and our attention was distracted by the fragile purple flames.

Party games were played after dinner, Adverbs and Charades; the less said about them the better. I managed to keep a low profile while everyone else made fools of themselves. Grandma released me for a while by asking me in a whisper to polish her riding boots. I assumed, from what Grandpa had said, that this was the kind of small eccentricity to be expected all the time now, and I did as I was asked. The shoe-cleaning box was in a cupboard in the pantry. The dogs watched me apply the brown polish with a cloth, relishing the smell of wax and turpentine as I did so. Then I brushed and buffed the old boots until they shone. I left them on a sheet of newspaper on the side, a pair of rescued trophies.

Back in the drawing room Grandpa offered everyone sloe gin he'd made: it conspired to taste both sickly sweet and horribly alcoholic, like all liquor; I poured mine into my father's glass when no one was looking.

By the time we got up to the attic it was clear that the twins had been knocking back their allocations of gin. Baz climbed into his alcove and asked why it was spinning, it was like being at a fairground. Xan asked Holly whether or not she had a G-spot.

'It does exist,' Baz affirmed.

'Our Dad told us,' said Xan.

'But not every woman's got one.'

Holly told them to mind their own business.

'Some women can have a vaginal orgasm and some women can't,' Baz said.

'What about you?' Xan demanded.

'Leave me alone,' Holly told them. She got up and turned off the main light; returning to her alcove she turned the one off in there. I did the same.

'You must know,' Baz said in the darkness, his voice a little higher than his brother's: Xan's was beginning to break.

'Unless she's a virgin,' Xan suggested.

'Don't be funny,' Baz told him. 'You know what kind of school she goes to.'

'Of course,' Xan agreed. 'Bog-standard.'

'Leave her alone,' I heard myself tell them.

'Ooh,' Xan cooed. 'Big Theo's standing up for his kissing cousin.'

'I mean it,' I said, emboldened by the fact that no one could see me.

'That's very gallant of him,' Baz said.

'Very butch,' said Xan.

'You know the dormer window up here?' I asked.

There was silence. Eventually, Xan asked, 'What about it?'

'If you two don't shut up and go to sleep I'm going to turn on the light and throw your iPod Touches out of that window.'

'You wouldn't dare,' Xan said.

'A drop of three floors straight on to the flagstones on the patio,' I said.

There was a longer silence, which extended, until it became clear from their drunken snoring that both twins had fallen asleep. Holly, though, was still awake.

'Theo,' she asked.

'Yes,' I said.

'Is Grandma really going to die?'

'We're all going to die,' I said.

'You know what I mean,' Holly said.

I wasn't sure what Holly wanted, or needed, me to say. 'Do you know what Grandpa told me today?' I asked. 'He said that the Venerable Bede, who wrote the first real history of England, well, Bede wrote, somewhere, that, "Life is the flight of a sparrow through the banquet hall." I asked Grandpa if that was what he thought: life is just this brief, insignificant flight. You know what he said?'

Holly sighed. 'What?' she said, and sniffed, the single syllable nasal and congested with her emotions.

'He said that for him the banquet hall is the mind of God. That's what we're gliding through.'

I didn't know whether Holly was thinking about what I'd just said. I wasn't sure I'd explained it properly. That this existence we're living in is itself the mind of God, which I thought at the time a startling idea. Then I realised that Holly was crying.

'I don't want Grandma to die,' she said.

'Neither do I,' I whispered. 'Neither do I.' I guess I welled up with emotion myself then. We drifted off to sleep in our alcoves, lamenting the mortality of those we loved, and most likely of ourselves.

IV

I

When I climbed out of my alcove on Boxing Day morning I turned and, before dressing, watched Holly and the twins: in a deep, heavy sleep, still and helpless. I felt old, suddenly, for an odd moment, looking down on these children.

Grandpa was standing well back from the kitchen window, binoculars raised. He stood beside Grandma, who sat in her warm chair by the Aga, with her mug of tea. She wore not her dressing gown as usual but tan jodhpurs and a white shirt. I kissed her good morning, she told me to make myself a drink.

Without lowering the field glasses, as he called them, my grandfather said, 'It's here, Theo.'

Beside him, Grandma shook her head.

'By the coach house,' Grandpa said. 'It'll be on the feeders in a moment.'

'Don't talk drizzle, Leonard,' Grandma said. She paused, her face blank, as if reviewing what had just emerged from her lips for an error she perceived dimly. Giving up on the search, she said, 'I don't know why you make such a fuss about your one ruddy woodpecker when other entire species are being forced from their habitat. How long are we going to see curlews here? Golden plover?'

Grandpa ignored her, and she turned to me. 'Did your grandfather tell you, Theo, that he didn't hear a cuckoo this spring?'

I had to admit that he hadn't, and shook my head.

'For the first time in his life. Is that not right, Leonard?' She had turned her attention back to her husband. 'So, just like you, the boy will simply watch the disappearing world. He'll suffer in a melancholy way. Who knows? Perhaps he'll write about it, another elegy for your library. But will he *do* anything?'

My grandmother's words, my grandfather's silence, too, had in them the history of other conversations, threaded back through their lives. Ancient conflicts, points where their personalities rubbed up against one another, returned to from new angles, in fresh contexts, year after year through their life together, even while Grandma's sickness brought a new febrility to her behaviour.

Grandpa stepped closer to the window, and scanned the landscape. He raised his gaze up the hill, and said, 'Jockie.' I looked too and saw a white blur up on the lane.

Grandma checked the clock on the wall above her. 'About time, too,' she said, and got up. By the time Jockie's Mini van had travelled down from the lane and around the house to the stable yard, my grandmother had donned her black jacket and was walking across the patio, carrying her riding boots in one hand and helmet in the other. She didn't walk like a frail old person, their bones turning brittle, but looked wiry and tough still, her back straight, her head held high. She'd given her last horse, Duncan, away that autumn (though she kept forgetting that she'd done so) with the proviso that she could borrow it on occasion. Grandpa explained to me now that he'd presumed no such occasion would arise.

'Forgot about Boxing Day,' he admitted. 'Not to mention your grandmother's bloody-mindedness. Nothing I could say to change her mind.' He lowered the binoculars for the first time, and shook his head. 'Seems to have disappeared,' he said regretfully.

I laid the table for breakfast. Uncle Jonny came in, saying, 'Stick the kettle on, Theo. Pa, I'll need to use your Internet after breakfast if I may. Bloody sight easier if you had wireless.'

'They only just got broadband,' I told my uncle, making a face to show him I understood how backward things were out here in the sticks.

Jockie had collected my grandfather's copy of *The Times* from the garage in the village, and my parents picked it up off the table in the hall on their way into breakfast. While Mum poured apple juice from a bottle in the fridge, Dad scanned the headlines.

'Oh, no,' he said.

'What is it?' Mum asked.

'Pinter's died.'

Uncle Jonny opened a mouth full of half-munched toast and said, 'Which one?'

'What do you mean, "Which one?"' my father said, coming over to the dining table. He was carrying the newspaper, as evidence, but maybe Jonny didn't realise that. 'Harold, of course.'

Uncle Jonny frowned. 'I don't remember any Harold. George was the one who played rugby, wasn't he?'

My father gazed at his brother, scrutinising his face for clues; to what, I wasn't sure. 'Harold Pinter,' he said. 'The playwright. Nobel prize. *No Man's Land. The Birthday Party.*'

Uncle Jonny gazed back at him, then nodded slowly. 'I thought you meant the Pinters of Cleobury North,' he said.

My mother broke open a hot roll. Butter melted. She added bilberry jam.

'That looks good,' Dad said. 'Give me a bite, Amy.'

'Make your own,' she said. Turning to Grandpa, she added, 'He always does this.'

'Because,' my father said, in his own defence, 'what you make always looks better. In fact, what anyone makes looks better, and it's all my father's fault. Whenever we went on a picnic Pa had the knack of knocking together delectable snacks. He'd spread a piece of bread with butter, break a chocolate bar up and put the bits on it, fold the bread over, you remember, Jonny, and there was this delicious chocolate sandwich.'

'So why didn't you just copy him?' Mum demanded.

'Too late,' Dad admitted. 'Pa would take ages getting everything ready, by which time I'd already eaten mine.'

Uncle Jonny looked at Mum and shook his head, glancing towards his brother, and said, 'Greedy bastard, he was.'

'Nineteen seventy-five,' Mum said, abruptly changing the subject. 'Or maybe seventy-six. My godmother had me to stay with her in Oxford on my own, for the first time, and took me to see *Otherwise Engaged* at The Playhouse.'

'What, a Pinter play?' Dad asked. 'I don't recall that one.'

'Simon Gray,' Mum said, 'but Harold Pinter directed, I remember. I must have been your age, Theo,' she said to me. 'Alan Bates played the main role, of this man trying to listen to a piece of music, who's endlessly interrupted, by a succession of maddening people. I remember it clearly,' she said. 'It was so exciting. Funny and foolish, but with other things going on I was aware of without understanding: the man's calm, and how long it could last. The whole evening, really. Taxi back to my godmother's house in Old Marston. You won't remember her,

Theo. It became a regular treat, staying with her, taken to the Playhouse.'

After breakfast Grandpa asked me to give the dogs a quick run. 'Take the field glasses,' he said. 'See if you can see him.'

The day was colder than it had been. The sky was filled with banks of cloud in differing tones of grey. With the earth in its winter hibernation, nature's smells were dormant, though not for the dogs: they tore hither and thither, the ground criss-crossed with the tracks of nocturnal animals. I walked beyond the coach house and the rusted machinery, past the swing ropes, up into the paddock above the riding school. Using the binoculars I found a buzzard on the hill, hovering high above the dead bracken, its gimlet eyes scrutinising the ground for movement. I scanned down, and there, in the magnified circle of the lens, appeared Aunt Lorna, jogging along the track that skirted the hill. She disappeared from sight, my view of her blocked by a grassy mound, but then reappeared down the path around it, running more freely now, letting herself go downhill. It wasn't easy to keep the binoculars on her, but I was determined to, right up until she filled the lens. Except a voice shattered the solitude of my voyeurism, making my heart thump; my arms dropped to my sides, the weighty binoculars cracked against my breastbone.

'She's beautiful, isn't she?'

It was Holly, who was looking not at me, as I'd feared, but up the hill. I gratefully handed her the binoculars. She raised them to her eyes. 'I wish I could be beautiful like her,' Holly said, as she adjusted focus. 'It's all double vision,' she said. 'I can't get it to go into one.'

'Just takes practice,' I mumbled.

She handed back the binoculars. 'Botox,' Holly said. 'Or Restylane. She has it done in New York.' There was an unmistakable tone of approval, or envy, in her voice. 'I've checked them on the Web. There's all sorts of injectables you can have. Oh, and Grandpa said to tell you we need to leave in a couple of minutes.'

I whistled for the dogs, and we turned towards the house. 'She talks to you about it?' I asked.

Holly shook her head. 'There's genetically engineered collagen,' she said. 'And they've just about eliminated allergic reactions.'

'Why are you so interested?' I asked.

Holly shrugged. 'I suppose I might have breast enlargement if they don't get bigger,' she said. She must have seen my reaction – I sensed her glance in my direction – because she added, 'Not now, I mean later. But the face. That's what everyone sees, right?'

I suppose I was shocked in part because I'd taken to heart my mother's opinion: that people who have cosmetic surgery are mentally ill, and the doctors who operate are criminals. 'But you,' I said. 'You're so . . .'

'So what?' Holly asked.

I heard noises up ahead, and glanced across the yard. My father was putting red buckets into the boot of Grandpa's car. Grandpa called to me, 'Put the dogs inside, would you, Theo?'

I watched my grey wellies clump along. I could feel my cheeks, despite the cold, glow red with unwanted heat.

'Pretty,' I said.

Holly laughed. 'You're just saying that,' she said, and ran towards the car.

2

Men – and women – of action cause the problems in this world, don't they? People with what are commonly called powerful personalities. Those who live a quiet life, on the other hand, tolerant of their fellows, adaptable to circumstance, capable of making an accommodation with the fugitive nature of love and the ephemeral fact of this fleeting existence; such individuals do little harm.

Yes, it is true that our children berate us for not having changed our ways sufficiently, forced others to change theirs. But the doers cause the problems, how are the thinkers to solve them? Even if they could turn themselves into doers, would they not then change their natures, and themselves create havoc? Of course they would.

This dualism, not between mind and matter but between changing the world and leaving it alone; this, it turns out, is the dichotomy embedded within the human species, which has gradually revealed itself over the course of history, unfurling like the tongue of some hideous serpent.

For hundreds of thousands of years survival kept the men of action busy enough, in hunting and war, while the rest were left to forage and gossip, to teach their children, to study healing herbs and intoxicants, to paint on the walls of caves, to make music. Technology has allowed the men of action to lay waste the world.

* * *

My father sat in the passenger seat, Holly and I in the back, as our grandfather drove us down to the large village to the east. Dad was telling Holly about a painting in the collection at Christ Church Picture Gallery, called *The Butcher's Shop*. 'It's an awfully strange painting,' he was saying, 'no one really knows what it means, but the human figures and the animal flesh are quite beautifully rendered. I think you'd like it.'

He spoke in such a way that made me think he knew more about art than I'd suspected. A private interest of his, kept separate from Mum and myself.

'Soutine's my total favourite,' Holly was telling him. 'My art teacher showed me this book.'

As we passed the first houses on the outskirts of the village, I noticed the car slow down a little. On our right-hand side was a *For Sale* notice outside a small, brick house, and Grandpa turned his head and peered at it as he drove by.

In the centre of the village lay the ruins of a castle built a thousand years earlier by one of the Marcher Lords. Little of the building remained, but the walls of the keep had been made good and the only entrance was through a great arched stone gateway, beside which my father and grandfather took up a position, each shaking a red bucket, saying, 'For the hunt staff,' to those who passed them.

Holly and I went on into the grassy keep. Almost as large as a cricket field, though bumpy and undulating, it was used for concerts and plays in the summer as well as the village fête, and various galas. Now people who'd driven from other villages around, cottages, outlying farms, as well as the inhabitants of the village itself, walked in, and milled around, greeting those they knew. Knots of people formed, their breath condensing in the cold Boxing Day morning, then unravelled and reformed in new clusters of conversation. Above, the cloud cover gave way to patches of clear blue sky, and quite suddenly the sun broke through, so that we had to shield our eyes, as we strolled around.

Horses and riders trotted in in dribs and drabs, in ones and twos. One woman held her reins in one hand, a mobile phone to her ear. The three hunt staff wore red jackets. They brought in the hounds and let them wander. All the other huntsmen and women wore black jackets, white jodhpurs, boots, except for one joker in a Santa Claus costume. There were some riders younger than Holly and I, on small ponies. They wore skullcaps. Most of the adults wore riding hats, the odd one a beagling hat. One or two had stuck Santa hats on top of their riding helmets; red and silver tinsel was wrapped around the bridles of their horses.

A short distance from us a horse became skittish, unsettled: it started wheeling around. People backed swiftly away, clearing a space around it. For a moment I thought that the rider, a middle-aged woman, speaking to her mount and pulling on its reins, was making the horse do this, as some sort of stunt or trick. But then I realised that she was attempting the opposite, trying to calm it down, which in time it did.

Everything was much bigger close-up. Holly and I went right up to a white horse whose rider towered above, and let us pat the animal's flanks. You couldn't feel its power from a distance, but up against its muscled flanks, its quivering strength, you could imagine what it must be like to be hurtled along on top of one, over hedges, ditches, out of control. The hounds, too, were long-legged, rangy creatures, loose-limbed. They roamed among the crowd, autonomous beings. I saw one pad up to a child in a buggy who held a rice cake in his hand: the hound snaffled it and carried on, loping along. The toddler stared into space for a long, horrified moment before bursting into tears.

'Look over there,' Holly said. A woman rider had come into the keep. Her face hidden behind a veil attached to her top hat, she wore a black jacket and a black skirt, and rode side saddle; she looked like the mysterious heroine of some provincial novel.

The keep had filled up, with riders and those on foot, when our grandmother rode slowly in. Duncan was a tall black horse, I don't know how many hands high. He'd been well groomed for the occasion: his mane was plaited tight to his spine, his sleek skin shone. He pranced through the crowd, his head high, and Grandma sat straight-backed aboard him. Other riders nodded to her, and she slowed Duncan to a stroll. Holly and I watched as people on foot came up to say hello. Some approached, only to stand some yards away and gaze at her, nodding if she caught their eye, before wandering off, somehow satisfied, whispering to each other.

Grandma wove a slow figure of eight through the crowd. The sense of anticipation that had been building was put on hold, all eyes upon her. She never looked so imperious to me, looking down upon the crowd from the great height of her mount, and although she did not deign to give so much as a smile to anyone, you could tell that she was happy.

'You know what's happening, don't you?' Holly whispered to me. I shook my head. Holly gestured towards our grandmother. 'They all know,' she said. 'People are saying goodbye.'

Riders began forming a line. People on foot moved towards the exit, and coalesced on either side. Then the Master of Hounds raised a trumpet to his lips and blew. The hounds jogged over from around the keep and followed him as he led the way out through the stone gateway. Behind them went the riders in a loose procession three or four abreast, out of the castle keep and on to the road, the horses' hooves clattering on the tarmac.

People made their way to their cars, parked higgledy-piggledy on grass verges, in the square, in front of the church. On the way home, driving out of the village, Holly asked Grandpa if he'd ever gone hunting.

'Me?' he said. 'Good God, no. Chase some poor vixen across the fields to watch her ripped to pieces by a pack of dogs? Not my idea of sport, Holly. I prefer to use a gun, which your grandmother calls a coward's weapon.' He laughed. 'You'd be more likely to find me with the hunt saboteurs. Like your uncle here.'

Holly was almost as excited as I was by this revelation. I'd never heard it before, but Dad admitted it was true.

'It's never been just a town-versus-country debate,' he said. 'The countryside's always been divided. But anyway, I never sabbed Ma's hunt.'

'But you've just collected money for the hunt staff,' I said, unable to fathom such hypocrisy.

'In case you youngsters hadn't noticed,' he said, 'they don't chase real live foxes any more. Nothing wrong with having a fun day out galloping around the countryside. Anyway, the truth is it means more to me to support Ma than oppose hunting.'

Holly asked Grandpa whether that was why he shook a red bucket.

'I've been following on foot all our married life,' he told her. 'I'd follow your grandmother through the gates of hell, if I could.' He looked into the rear-view mirror, caught my gaze; perhaps Holly's too. 'You should have seen her forty years ago,' he said. 'You wouldn't find a braver horseman in this county.

She was the Field Master, she had a hundred riders behind her.' He shook his head. 'What a sight she was, leading the charge. Magnificent. The people around here revere her, you know. As they did her father.'

We sat in silence, as the car climbed the lane up the hill. As do you, Grandpa, I thought. Our grandfather had built his business up from nothing, and become a wealthy, respected, powerful man. It was his wealth, after all, that had allowed our grandmother to live the way she did. But if you didn't know that when you saw him and Grandma together you'd never guess, so modestly did he defer to her.

We were driving around the garden, below the house, when Holly said, 'She won't ride with the hounds today, will she, Grandpa?'

Our grandfather brought the car to a halt in the yard, across from the empty stables, and switched off the engine. He shook his head. 'I had a word with one or two people,' he said, with a kind of quiet certainty that made me question my assumption of a moment before, and wonder about their relationship all over again, and where the power lay between them.

'Even if she tries,' Grandpa said, 'and I wouldn't put it past her, despite her promise to me, they won't let her. Don't worry. Not now.'

3

'Actually, Grandma,' said Baz, 'this is a really weird family.'
We were all having lunch, spinach soup with rolls.

'Exactly,' Xan agreed.

'The sons have had sons,' Baz continued, 'and the daughter's had daughters.'

'Just look around the table,' Xan suggested.

I saw Gwen, and her two girls; Jonny and his two boys; my father, and myself. 'Wow,' I said.

'That's incredible,' said Holly.

'Don't be ridiculous,' Grandma said. 'What about Matt?'

Holly's mouth assumed the shape of an O of embarrassment that she'd forgotten her own brother.

Baz was unfazed. 'He doesn't count.'

'No,' Xan agreed.

'He's not here.'

'He will be,' Grandma declared with utter, misplaced confidence in her prodigal grandson. She made no effort to conceal the fact that Matt was her clear favourite, just as Jonny, according to my father, had enjoyed this status when they were growing up, something he and Gwen had accepted: the younger brother could do no wrong. His every achievement was met with lavish praise, his misdemeanours with indulgence. I knew this strand of the fabric of our family myth, but it seemed to have unravelled since: Grandma appeared to treat her now middle-aged children with equal measures of affection and disdain, Uncle Jonny no longer his mother's golden boy.

Matt had taken over this position, apparently pretty well from the moment he was born, the first of Grandma's grandchildren, and neither his sisters nor the rest of his cousins, myself included, minded, as far as I could tell: I came here every summer, yet knew a postcard from Matt meant more to our grandmother than my month-long presence, and was unbothered by her heart's irrational preference.

'I'm not sure Mattie will be coming now, Ma,' Auntie Gwen, Matt's mother, sighed. 'It's Boxing Day already.'

At that very moment, unbelievably, we heard the blast of a horn. A car was coming down the drive, on the blind side of the house from where we were sitting at the dining-room table. The twins rose from their seats in unison, and leaped to the window behind them.

'Sports car,' said Xan. 'Classic.'

'Red,' Baz stated. 'Triumph.'

'Spitfire,' Xan suggested.

'Precisely,' Baz agreed.

'Mattie,' trilled Sidney, rising from the table herself.

I don't think I was the only one to look at Grandma then. Her face was suffused with a kind of joyful vindication, which I have fixed in my memory, with the sound not of others pushing their chairs back, chattering excitedly – these have vanished, in truth, and return only as I summon them now through a decisive act of will – but with a sound which was in the background: that of the deep-throated growl of Matt's vintage sports car as it swung into the yard, and then additional guttural roars as he gunned the throttle before switching off the engine. My grandmother, I thought, looked imperious, gracious, truly happy.

It was quite curious what ensued: most of those at the table rushed outside to greet my long-awaited cousin – their son, grandson, brother, nephew. Because of this very eagerness of theirs, perhaps, mixed with my own shyness, I felt a certain reluctance to do so myself. He's taken so long to get here, I thought, why should we all interrupt our meal and run to him? Let him come to us! Then I realised that the only other two people who'd remained at the lunch table were my own parents. A momentary spasm of pride and solidarity, during which we smiled at each other in, I assumed, shared acknowledgement, was followed by a gut-sagging sense of disappointment. Yes, the mean-minded Oxonians remained in their seats, unlike those outgoing inhabitants of the capital who generously acclaimed their relative's arrival.

Was I doomed, by genetic inheritance, by a gloomy temperament, to be forever on the outside, a spectator of events? A cloistered academic? A chronicler; the one who relates the tale, set forever apart from the action, the story itself, that arena occupied by heroes and heroines? To be aloof from one's own life: what a sentence.

Matt came towards the house, the others swarming around him. I watched through the window. No one was carrying his bags; in the excitement they all seemed to have left them in the car. As they came into the kitchen we three finally stood up, and Matt stepped over to kiss my mother, and hug my father, 'Uncle Rod!', and shake my hand, telling the assembled company, 'He's almost as tall as I am!'

Matt had blond-brown hair, a small nose, generous lips, brown eyes, just like Holly; but he was incredibly handsome; her slight flaws had been made perfect in him. His eyes were dazzling, his teeth were unblemished. It was as if when Holly came along nature tried to copy what it had achieved with her brother, but narrowly failed. He wore a T-shirt under an unbuttoned shirt, loose jeans, a beaded necklace, a bracelet on one wrist. His hair appeared bleached. Matt looked as if on this English winter's day in the middle of the countryside he was just about to go surfing.

Matt's mother and sisters fluttered around him like hand-maidens, collaborating to meet his every whim: soup, roll, a glass of beer; knife, spoon, plate, bowl. Even the twins regarded him without their customary cynicism, but watched him eagerly.

'Do give me your place, Jonny,' Matt demanded of his uncle. 'I want to sit next to Grandma.'

'Move along,' Grandma told her son, and she sat beaming at Matt as he ate.

'How long are you staying?' Baz asked him.

'He's here now, that's all that matters,' Grandma told the assembled company, holding Matt's left hand in hers. 'Here to stay.'

'I have more care to stay than will to go,' he said, squeezing Grandma's hand.

I heard my mother murmur under her breath, 'More light and light it grows.'

It occurred to me then that, alone among all of us, Matt knew nothing yet of Grandma's illness. Except, I reflected, Auntie Gwen would surely have phoned to tell him?

I still have, somewhere, the single-page programme Holly and I typed out on our grandfather's computer, down in his study, for the concert our parents obliged us to perform that afternoon. I took photos with my new paparazzo camera, in which Sid, Holly, Xan and Baz each posed as if caught unawares; Xan did the same for me, and we uploaded them on to the computer, and printed them, as thumbnails, on the programme.

The concert was dedicated to our grandmother, but actually there was a list of people thanked for one reason or another which included every member of the audience: our respective parents, of course, for music lessons paid for; our grandfather, for hosting the occasion; as well as Matt, 'for coming'. This last was my suggestion, by the way, but Holly took it as a thoughtful contribution and typed it up, rather missing the irony in my tone of voice.

We performed in order of age, starting with the eldest, Sidney, partly because she was prepared to go first 'into the lions' den', as she put it, but also because we figured the audience – their patience tested by the standard of our playing, even given the planned brevity of the concert – might be more self-indulgent the younger the musician. Grandma sat in her chair by the open fire, pine logs burning, with Matt sitting on the floor, leaning back against the front of her chair beside Grandma's legs, her hand resting on his shoulder, his hand across his chest resting on hers. Grandpa sat in his chair on the other side of the fire, turned so that he could see the piano in the corner of the room. My parents, uncle and aunts sat on the sofa and chairs, which we'd configured into a crescent from Grandma's chair around to the window, in front of the Christmas tree.

With Holly as her page-turner, Sidney took her seat at the baby grand piano. She turned to the audience and said, 'I'm going to play *Rose's Theme* by James Horner.' She peered at the sheet music, as if to make sure it was the right one, then turned back to the grown-ups. 'He wrote it for the film *Titanic*, starring Leonardo di Caprio and Kate Winslett. It's the theme tune. So you might recognise it.' She peered again at the music, screwing up her eyes and leaning forward. It can't have been easy to play with her torso at that angle, her weight pressing forward into her arms, but she launched bravely into the wash of notes. Whether anyone would have recognised it, except as a vaguely familiar dirge, is unlikely. Sid's fingers appeared to be stubby digits tentatively connected to her mind, tapping indelicately, perfunctorily, on the keys of the pianoforte, rather as if she were typing the tune rather than playing it, like a journalist in an old black-and-white movie. It was what my mother called plinketty-plonketty piano: you felt that whoever Sid's teacher was had drummed into her that the most important thing was the beat: Sid nodded her head like a metronome as she played, keeping herself in time.

When she'd finished, Sid stood up and took a bow, facing the audience with her left hand stretched out and touching the piano still like a professional, an artist unwilling yet to relinquish their physical union with the instrument. The applause was raucous. Uncle Jonny yelled, 'Superb! Bravo!' Matt put two fingers in his mouth and whistled. Auntie Gwen had tears in her eyes, whether moved more by the music or her daughter's moment in the spotlight I wasn't sure. My parents and Aunt Lorna on the sofa clapped politely.

Holly, one month older than me, was up next, and she began by giving a potted history of her instrument, the saxophone. 'A wind instrument made of brass,' she explained, 'possessing woodwind characteristics.' It was invented by Adolphe Sax, she informed us, born in Belgium, died in Paris, France, in 1894. There were twelve members of the saxophone family, apparently, the most popular and recognisable being the large tenor sax. 'Mine is an alto,' Holly explained. 'Like the others, it has twenty keys, which control the notes.' She carried on describing the ways in which a saxophone was similar to or different from an oboe, and a clarinet, but not for much longer. She'd gone over her introduction with me earlier, and I'd advised her to curtail it. The audience, I said, would be eager to hear her play. Now, as she began to perform her first piece, Glenn Miller's 'In the Mood', I realised how wrong I'd been. Everyone would have emptied their pockets to have her carry on talking as long as possible. Holly was an even worse musician than her sister. Each note she blew was separate, adrift, from the one before and the one that came after. There was no flow, and thus no tune, just a series of blasts that sounded as if they came from a wounded beast. With indigestion. I actually feared that anyone at all musical, like Mum, might be forced to clap their hands over their ears, because the volume of each elephant blast was truly impressive. Holly could have performed in the coach house and we'd have heard her perfectly well. She must have had unnaturally strong lungs inside her thirteen-year-old frame; should have been a hill runner, a deep-sea diver, rather than the blower of a wind instrument in this limited domestic space.

When she finished, the last note died with a sigh of relief, and Holly herself took a deep breath and announced that she was going to also play 'Au Clair de la Lune' by Claude Debussy. My mother's blank expression amounted to an act of heroic self-control.

How low and confined is our self-concern. As Holly took Debussy apart, note by painful note, and I noticed the dogs slink from the room, I took pleasure in the prospect of how well received my own offering would be, following what had gone before. I was an efficient rather than a natural musician, and I'd rehearsed the piece I was going to play on my guitar until I had it note perfect.

'I'm going to perform one of the studies, the *études*, of Matteo Carcassi,' I said. 'Opus sixty, number twenty-five.' I played the piece as well as I'd ever played it, stood up, took a bow holding the guitar by its neck, acknowledged my family's gratitude for my melodic competence.

The twins had instructed us to put *to be confirmed* under the title of their piece in the programme. I'd presumed they were still arguing about what they'd perform. Now Xan set up a karaoke machine, while Baz told everyone that, 'We wanted to do something authentic. From the street.' They couldn't announce the material in advance as there were 'copyright issues', and that this was to be a 'guerrilla performance'.

' "Mess Wiv Me",' Baz said, 'was written by N-Kay and featured Darren Baker and Zinc. It came out this year and went straight to number one on the underground chart. To help you get a handle on it, this song mixes N-Kay's Grime style with dance rhythms from Darren and an R&B flavour from Zinc.' He turned to his brother and said, 'Hit it.'

What followed I find difficult to describe. My twin twelve-year-old cousins took on the personae of hip-hop gangsters: they each went into a kind of mistrustful slouch, using their whole bodies to augment a surly expression; at the same time, they both appeared to try to be seductive to the womenfolk in the room.

'If you're lookin' at me you better be sure,' Xan rapped.

'Give me the eye better know what for.'

Baz came in on the end of each line, his voice adding emphasis.

'Take one look cos you know I can *make it*
Waste my time? You know that I *hate it*
Come on to me, you better not *fake it*
So give it up, girl,
cos you know that I'll *take it*.'

What made the performance particularly authentic, one gathered, were the lewd gestures the boys made with their bodies. Xan spent most of the song with one hand on his crotch, the other pointing at his grandmother, or one of his aunts.

'Mess wiv me you mess wiv my bruvver
In a tight spot we back up each uvver
Share the blood, the trouble, the fee,
Mess wiv my bruvver you mess wiv me.'

Baz's favoured move was to hold one hand to the back of his head, the other on his stomach, and to bump and grind his groin. It was a hideous spectacle, my cousins' pubescent sexual contortions in our grandparents' drawing room. I could feel myself sweating with embarrassment, knew my hot cheeks were flushing crimson. Yet no one objected. Grandma gazed vacantly, as she had through everything else. What the others thought I couldn't imagine, but when this repulsive performance came to an end they applauded cheerfully. Even the twins' own parents appeared unabashed.

Afterwards, two of the adults, Mum and Auntie Gwen, fetched tea and chocolate cake as a reward for our efforts.

'Why have you got this piano, anyway?' Holly asked Grandpa. 'Mum doesn't play. Do you, Uncle Rod?' she asked my father.

'We're all cloth-eared,' Uncle Jonny proclaimed, in no way ashamed.

'Tone-deaf,' Auntie Gwen regretted.

'Ma forced us all to have lessons,' Dad said. 'We each of us gave up as soon as we could.'

'Not a moment too soon,' said Grandpa, the first words he'd uttered all afternoon, which made them sound all the more heartfelt, and allowed the pretence and tension in the room to escape in laughter.

4

Sidney collected tea cups and plates and carried them away on a large tray. Auntie Gwen requested volunteers to help her in the kitchen. Lorna put herself forward and told the twins to come too. Matt climbed to his feet and said, 'Dear, dear, is that the time already? What a fabulous afternoon we've all had. However much it pains me, better hit the road before darkness falls.'

A sense of shock rippled through the room. Our cousin had only arrived a couple of hours earlier, and he was leaving already? I imagine we must all have looked towards our grandmother then. I know I did.

'Now the rest of you lot stay here,' Matt said. He blew kisses around the room. 'It's been wonderful to catch you all, but I want Grandma to see me off. Just the two of us.'

From the kitchen I watched him head towards his car, Grandma leaning on his arm as she had on mine in the church-yard. They shared a long embrace, and then Matt lowered himself into the red sports car, gunned the engine, reversed in the yard and pulled away. Grandma watched him disappear from view and then stood with her head bent to the ground, lost in thought or perhaps listening still to the sound of the car's growl as it climbed the drive on the other side of the house, and faded along the lane. She turned, eventually, and started walking back towards the house. Halfway across the patio she stumbled, and steadied herself against the picnic table. My mother rushed out, and escorted her in.

Mum and Dad persuaded Grandma to take a rest and let the others get on with it. She agreed to 'put her feet up', not in bed but in front of the television. My parents had given her a DVD set of the BBC natural history series *Planet Earth*, and the three of them went through and watched the first episode. As I went past them, back to the drawing room, Dad was putting a blanket over her lap.

Holly and I put our instruments back in their cases, and shifted furniture back to its original configuration.

'I had no idea you were such a good guitarist, Theo,' Holly said. 'You've been keeping that quiet.'

'I write my own songs,' I said, shrugging modestly.

'With lyrics and everything?' Holly was aghast. 'What about?'

'Oh, you know, war and stuff.'

'Why didn't you sing one?' she demanded.

'I don't really perform in public,' I blushed. 'Working in a studio's more nang than live performance.'

'You've actually made recordings?'

'Not exactly,' I admitted. 'Not yet. I might video something. Post it on YouTube.'

'Get on MySpace,' Holly said. 'Hey. We should play together.'

'Yeah,' I drawled, as slowly as I could, then frowned. 'I'm just not sure there are many pieces for sax and guitar.'

'Really?' said Holly. 'That's such a shame.'

I nodded. 'It's a bummer.'

'Wait,' she said. 'I know. Why don't you write something?'

The twins were laying the table, arguing over whether to put a dessert spoon and fork beside or above the place mat; and if the former, then inside or outside the other cutlery.

Auntie Gwen poured a layer of fried vegetables into a large dish and Aunt Lorna laid rectangles of pasta across them.

'It's my favourite chair,' Auntie Gwen said, watching Lorna's elegant fingers lay down the brittle snaps of lasagne.

'Yes,' Lorna said. 'It's a good chair.'

'But don't you see? It's mine,' Gwen said. 'It always was.'

'One of the few pre-Victorian pieces in the entire house,' Lorna said. 'I'm pretty certain it's a William the Fourth library chair. With those turned and fluted supports. The shaped back and arms.'

'But I don't care when it was *made*, or what it's worth.' Auntie Gwen poured in more vegetables. Courgette, carrot, aubergine. 'I just don't understand why Jonny put a first priority sticker on it.'

Lorna flattened the mixture in the dish with a fork. 'He didn't,' she said. 'I did.' She turned towards the Aga, where Sid was stirring the contents of a large saucepan with a wooden spoon in one hand, holding a book she was reading with the other. 'That bechamel sauce ready yet?' Lorna asked. 'All I'm doing,' she said, turning back to Auntie Gwen, 'is playing by the rules your parents set. That's not a problem, is it?'

When she caught sight of me watching her, Aunt Lorna seemed not in the least surprised, but smiled at me, very slightly raised her eyebrows, and said, 'Theo, darling, why don't you see if your grandmother would like a cup of tea.'

It wasn't easy to interrupt the television spectators: my grandmother ignored my whispered enquiry, until Dad found the remote and paused the DVD. Grandma dismissed my offer with so peremptory a shake of her hand that I might have been suggesting a gram of hard drugs. 'Do take these dogs out, Theo,' she said instead. 'I don't know where Leonard's got to. If they're not getting under horses' feet, they're getting under mine.'

The dogs attacked each other playfully as we crossed the patio, and the yard. There was a faint smell of woodsmoke: one of Jockie's bonfires, still smouldering; he'd turned it over after he'd dropped Grandma back after the Boxing Day meet in the castle that morning. The beautiful cold blue day was dying, the sun a crimson globe setting beyond the Welsh mountains. I heard a sound like a solid drum: a woodpecker. I took the dogs down into the wood.

Apart from a scattered handful of Scots pines – planted, Grandpa had explained, for winter colour – all the trees were deciduous: a central core of English oak, and ash ('the wood that's used for all that trim on the outside of your car', he'd told me, gesturing towards our Morris Traveller); surrounded with birch, rowan, crab apple and wild cherry. These trees were leafless now, dormant, their leaves rotting into the earth around them, a mulch to inhibit other plants stealing the soil's nutrients, as well as providing some of their own. Walking among the trees I studied the ground, as Grandpa had shown me, identifying a badger's habitual trail; the feathers of a crow flown up to its roost too late, caught and eaten by a fox; the droppings of deer, rabbit. It was strange that animals Grandpa was prepared to shoot came deep into his territory; he'd claimed that it was precisely because he culled and kept their numbers down that his land remained fruitful for them, but at that time I couldn't quite understand how.

I did decide, however, that I wanted to live near, or preferably within, a wood. Perhaps even, it occurred to me then, this very one. I didn't even need the house: the others – my cousins, our parents – could share that, while I built myself a treehouse down here.

It was some years ago now that I heard that the wood had been cut down, for firewood.

On my way back I noticed light from a window of Grandpa's workshop. Figuring someone must have left it on, I entered the outbuildings by a door further along the wall. You can see out of doors perfectly well for long after you need illumination indoors, so that I was surprised by the darkness, and had to feel my way slowly through a dim room where potatoes were stored. The smell, of musky earth, was so strong I felt like I was underground, like a mole in its lair. Just as I reached the door into the workshop, a voice began speaking on the other side. Whoever it belonged to must have been pondering something in silence, or maybe listening on the phone, while I'd groped my way towards him.

'I just need to pay off the interest on the loan or they've got me by the balls,' a voice I now recognised as Uncle Jonny's said. He must, it occurred to me, be speaking into his profanity phone. 'I feel like a twat,' he said. 'So what do I do? Bend over and take it up the arse? No fucking way. I'll come back at them and hit the bastards twice as hard as they hit me.'

'How long do you have?' a second voice asked, which surprised me.

'Eight days,' Uncle Jonny replied. 'It's just this month. Next month, I guarantee, I'll be back into profit, this is just a weird fucking blip. Rod and Gwen don't even need to know.'

'I find it hard to believe how stupid you've been,' the second person said. I realised now that it was Grandpa.

'Your mistake,' Uncle Jonny said, 'is to think the landscape is in *any* way comparable to the way it was. In your day. Jesus Christ. These are not some country fucking squires we're dealing with.' There was silence, before Jonny added, 'Anyhow, no one could have predicted this.'

'*Everyone* did,' Grandpa said.

There was another long pause then. Perhaps they'd been here ever since the music recital, conversing in this stark, staccato way: brief bouts of argument and insult, interspersed with long, belligerent silences.

'When you retired –'

'Retired?' Grandpa interrupted. 'I didn't retire. I had practically no orchards left. Got out with a little money because we scrubbed them up, and managed to sell the land for other use. You have no idea what it did to me, Jonny.'

Once again neither spoke for a while.

'In ten years this amateurish industry of ours had been killed off by an invasion, container ships with their refrigerated holds full of bland, shiny, tasteless apples, each and every one the same identical size.'

'Oh, spare us the self-pitying reminiscence. We all know what you did to accumulate those orchards in the first place. Bought out that old fart down the border. That's what we do, men like you and I, we make things happen. We see opportunity and have the balls to chase it.'

A further silence, heavy with threat and tension.

'They're your fucking grandsons,' Uncle Jonny said at last. 'That is who we're trying to protect. You can't deny that, you mean old bastard.'

The pause this time was shorter. 'What about Lorna's family? Won't –'

'Can you not under*stand*?' Jonny interrupted, his voice much louder, almost shouting at his father. 'There's nothing else. It's all crumbling. Lorna? Her family have nothing. They never did. What, you still think she's from the Argentine aristocracy? She was a dancer in a fucking club, Pa. That's where I found her. She reinvented herself. There's nothing there.'

'I didn't realise.'

Rather more quietly, Uncle Jonny said, 'She's had a good look at a bungalow down the hill, by the way. Rather lovely, she reckoned.'

'I know,' Grandpa said.

I retreated carefully through the darkness, found the door latch, quietly raised it and let myself out. The dogs had disappeared; gone to the back of the house, probably, waiting there for someone to let them in. I walked along the side wall of the outbuilding. Just before I reached the corner, I heard the door of the workshop open, then close. Footsteps rapped on the concrete. Grandpa came into view, just a few metres away from me, his tightly hunched figure stumping angrily away towards the house. And he was muttering to himself in a way that shook me to my core.

About a year before the events herein described took place, my father took me with him to a spiritualist church in Oxford. In Summertown, not far from where we lived. 'For research,' he explained to me as we walked along Squitchey Lane, although I'm not sure that what we witnessed that day ever made it into one of his classes. Perhaps the visit was meant for my education, as well as his own amusement.

The visiting medium, a middle-aged man from Swindon, told

us that in order to make contact with our deceased forbears he would let his spirit guide come and take over his body. He closed his eyes and as we watched him an amazing transformation took place in front of our eyes: his features sagged and drooped, ageing him by ten or twenty years; his face became that of someone else; I could have sworn that there was even some alteration in the colour of his skin. It was utterly incredible, like something Hollywood special effects people spent millions of dollars on, but there it was, happening for real, in front of me.

The medium slowly opened his eyes, and spoke to us in the deep voice of an old Indian man – 'with a Peter Sellers accent', according to Dad – and proceeded to pass on invaluable pieces of information, and useful advice, to people in the congregation from their loved ones now residing in the spiritual realm.

The extraordinary thing was that the man's incredible metamorphosis was authentic, sincere. As my father said afterwards, if he was fooling us he was also fooling himself: he clearly believed in what he was doing, or having done to him.

And the reason I'm relating this anecdote is to give an idea of how shocked I was when I heard my grandfather walking away from the workshop that Boxing Day afternoon, cursing loudly. 'You gives it away and it's gone, ain't it? There be no bloody fool like an old fool.' Because he did so speaking in a way I'd never heard him, with a broad Salopian accent; the accent, I realised, of his early, long ago childhood.

I waited until Grandpa had gone inside the house, and then I waited a little longer, for Uncle Jonny to go in, too. There was a line of burnished orange along the black horizon. When I finally walked across the yard, there was an orange glow ahead of me, on the patio. I smelled the cigarette smoke, and realised who it was – muttering to himself, typically – before I reached him. When I spoke, my father jumped; the shock made him cough. He asked me what I was doing.

'I was walking the dogs,' I said. Then I realised someone else was there too, beside Dad. Wrapped up in a coat she hugged tight to herself, it took me a moment to make out it was Aunt Lorna. I was going to say I didn't know she was a smoker, too, but then my father told me the dogs were already inside when he came out.

'The temptation is to linger though, Theo, isn't it?' he said. 'Especially when it's so still. It's easy to imagine the nocturnal world coming to life all around us. Even if it is bloody cold.' He threw the butt of his rollie into a bush. 'Shall we go in?' he asked, addressing Aunt Lorna and me both.

It was my father's idea to play games after our early supper, and with the promise of cards with the adults later on, Oh Hell and Racing Demon, we children began with Sardines. The simple rules were that one person would hide, the others would look for him or her; if you found him you would join him in his hiding place; the game continued until all but one of the searchers had found the hiding place, and squeezed in like sardines. The game finished when the last person found all the others, whereupon he or she was pronounced the loser, and had then to be the hider in the next game.

I volunteered to go first, after I had a sudden inspiration: when I'd stayed during the summer in Grandpa's dressing room, I'd noticed that his built-in wardrobe was almost a walk-in one, a veritable closet. It was not only ten or twelve feet wide but also just as deep, much deeper than you could possibly have guessed from the other dimensions of the room. Like some magic trick, it was as if a cavity in the centre of the building had been conjured out of nothing.

While Sidney, Holly, Xan and Baz pretended to close their eyes, sat around the dining table, and count to fifty, I trod silently in my socks upstairs, made my way to the room and pushed through the hanging coats, jackets, trousers and shirts. Although the floor of the wardrobe was covered in neatly paired shoes, it wasn't difficult for me to make room for myself by turning one pair of brown leather brogues around – so that they were pointing out towards the door rather than back towards the wall – and stepping into them. They were just about the right size for me. Clothes were stacked loosely along the rails. I pushed them forward, closed the wardrobe doors, which clicked satisfyingly shut, stood against the back wall, and waited in the darkness.

The comforting smell of my grandfather's old clothes was mixed with that of naphthalene, or camphor, found in moth-balls, a faint aroma of which permeated everything. I didn't know what caused this smell – didn't think I'd ever come across it before – but whenever I have encountered it on odd occasions since I have been plummetted back into the wardrobe, and what happened next, that Christmas of my childhood.

My wristwatch had a little button on the side, which if pressed switched on a light that illuminated the watch face, enabling one to tell the time in the dark. After eleven and a quarter minutes I heard someone open the doors of the wardrobe, rustle around a little and then, to my disappointment, step inside. Perhaps they'd spotted my ankles, in a gap between the shoes and the bottom of the coats. He or she then closed the door behind them. The wardrobe was once more plunged into total darkness, but now there was someone else in there with me, shifting position, shuffling their feet amongst the shoes on the floor, and breathing. I stood as still as I possibly could for as long as I could stand it, breathing through my wide open mouth. But as the other person grew quieter, it became more difficult for me to breathe silently. I seemed to need to take ever deeper breaths, partly out of annoyance with this fool who gave no indication of being aware of my presence. I wondered whether he or she did, in fact, know that I was in there: perhaps they thought that *everyone* was supposed to hide, and it was a total coincidence that we were both in this same enclosed space.

I became convinced that this other person could hear me breathing, even as he or she became ever more silent. Then I began to doubt whether they were there or not, whether anyone else had actually climbed into the wardrobe at all. Maybe I'd imagined the whole thing. I knew that, robbed of sight, the human imagination could do strange things to its possessor, and that under stress the mind was prone to hallucinate. Eventually I could take it no more, and demanded, in a fierce whisper, 'Who's there?'

There was no reply. Silence. I could feel my pulse racing in the darkness now, my heart pulsating. 'I know you're there,' I rasped once more. 'Who are you?'

A hushed voice I recognised immediately as Holly's replied, 'I knew you'd be in here, Theo.'

What nonsense! Anger flared through me. 'How?'

'Oh, you've been banging on about how much you like staying in Grandpa's dressing room, and no one else ever does, what a privilege.' It was strange: it was impossible to tell where Holly's voice came from: whether to the left, or the right, or directly in front. 'I knew you'd come straight up here, and as soon as I came into the room I knew you'd be in this wardrobe.'

'Rubbish.'

'It was obvious. Had to be.'

With creaks of coat hangers and then scrapes of shoes, Holly started to move in the darkness. I couldn't tell where she was coming from, or shifting position to. I raised my watch, pressed the button and swept my wrist in an arc ahead of me, from left to right. Turning, I found myself face to face with the grinning visage of my cousin, bathed in a dim, green light. I regret to say that I'm prepared to admit I may have let slip a slight sound of surprise. The light went off.

Once my heart had stopped banging against my chest, and Holly had finished sniggering, I said, 'If you came straight here, how come it took you almost twelve minutes?'

'I had to make sure,' she replied, with irritating logic, 'that none of the others knew where I was.'

We stood in silence, side by side. We were almost touching. I became aware of Holly's slow breathing, and adjusted my own to fit hers, inhaling, resting, exhaling. It began to amuse me, wondering whether she realised what I was doing. Then I became aware of her smell amongst the cotton and wool and camphor, a subtle perspiring sweetness. I felt myself lean imperceptibly closer to her in the pitch-black darkness.

'Shhh!' Holly suddenly uttered in my ear – though I'd said nothing for some minutes – and the next thing I knew the doors of the wardrobe were opened. What happened next took me a moment to fathom: I was assailed by something; something malleable, corporeal, alive; being applied to my face. After some seconds I realised what it was: Holly had put her hand over my mouth.

I could hear Xan's voice, 'No, they're not here,' and Baz saying, 'Are you sure? Have another look.' The jackets and coats ruffled in front of me, and in the semi-darkness I saw Xan's hand reach in, and float around, and withdraw.

I was preoccupied, meanwhile, with how infuriating the situation was. There was no need whatsoever for Holly, after she'd hushed me, to have put her hand on my mouth, and keep it there, where it presently remained. But once she'd done so there was nothing I could do about it without giving myself, us, away. If I'd grabbed her hand and wrestled it loose, no doubt there'd have been a commotion; and if I'd muttered and hummed noises of objection the twins would have heard. So I stood there, mute, passive – as if thereby acknowledging, indeed, the necessity of her maddening intervention.

'Nothing,' said Xan.

Behind him, Baz said, 'I bet he's in the attic like I said. We just missed him the first time. Come on.'

'Sid and Holly must have both found him,' Xan said, as he closed the door.

After some moments I took hold of Holly's wrist and tried to pull it away. She resisted at first, whispering, 'They might be listening.'

We struggled for a moment, until I felt her relinquish her hand.

'Why the hell did you do that?' I demanded.

Her voice sounded nonchalant in the darkness. 'I was worried you might squeak again,' she said.

Blood rushed to my head. 'How would you like it?' I asked, and put my left hand over her mouth. Somewhat to my surprise, Holly didn't resist, but let my hand rest on her mouth, and we stood there like that for some time. My anger subsided. It ebbed away in the midst of confusion as I felt Holly's lips open, and her tongue emerge, and taste the skin of my middle finger. I stood there, motionless, as Holly proceeded to explore my fingers with her tongue; and then her moist lips, kissing them; and then her teeth, with which she bit me.

I didn't exactly decide upon a course of action, it was more that I experienced myself having apparently begun to move my head around to face Holly's, and at the same time withdraw my hand from her mouth. A moment later I discovered myself kissing her, and being kissed by her. My innards turned to liquid, my head filled with air. The bodily pleasures I would have regarded as supreme in my experience of life hitherto were rendered insignificant, facile, by the delicious sensations I now discovered.

It was Holly Simmons, my cousin, but it felt like I was getting to know a complete stranger in an entirely novel way, one which the two of us invented as we explored together, a pair of young gods.

No one disturbed us again for a long time, and we continued our mutual exploration with little pause. I think, looking back, that even as we indulged in this delectable game, which neither of us had planned, we knew already that it could go no further. There was no anxiety about whether or when or how another step should be taken. Perhaps it was for this reason that a pattern of my sexual destiny was laid down in that darkness: an enjoyment of kissing for its own sake, not merely as something that leads to something else.

Eventually, one of us – I think it was Holly, though it could have been me – said that we ought to make our way downstairs.

The others had probably all given up on us by now, we agreed, forgotten our very existence and were no doubt in the middle of a game of Racing Demon.

I opened the wardobe door – which, fortunately, was possible from inside. The light was on in Grandpa's dressing room. For a moment it seemed blinding. When I was able to look at Holly, who was smiling at me, I saw that something had changed. The flaws in her appearance – her cross-eyes, her snub nose, uneven teeth – had shifted, improved. She was prettier than she had been an hour earlier. My kissing, for which I clearly had a natural talent, had made her more attractive. I knew, of course (I wasn't stupid) that what had happened was that I had made her *feel* attractive, and that this was enough, this self-belief, to make it a reality.

It didn't occur to me that what had shifted was my own perception, though as we walked through our grandparents' bedroom and out on to the landing I did realise that Holly putting her hand over my mouth had made me forget the rules of the game: the whole point of Sardines was for everyone to gather in a hiding place. I should really have taken hold of Xan's hand and pulled him in.

We came downstairs and found everyone in the drawing room, not playing cards, as we'd expected, but sitting and standing in odd poses all around the room, in silence, like brooding statues. They didn't see us at first, but when one did so all the others came swiftly to animated life.

My father turned towards me and said, 'Where the hell have you been?'

'Didn't you hear the siren?' Xan demanded.

I realised now that some were missing from the company.

'Grandma's been taken to hospital,' Sidney said. 'She had a fall.'

'The doctor came,' my mother explained, 'and said she needed to be kept under observation.'

Dad told Holly that her mother had gone with Grandpa to the hospital. Everyone was staring at us. Holly burst into tears. I almost did the same, overwhelmed by the accumulation of shock, guilt, sadness all at once. My mother went over and gave Holly a hug. She held her for a long time, soothing her, and rubbing her back in a way I recognised immediately, not from sight but because I could feel the place down my own spine from when she did the same to me. It also occurred to me, perhaps for the first time, that my mother would have loved to have had a daughter.

Our grandfather and Auntie Gwen got back from Shrewsbury shortly after eleven. The twins had gone to bed; Holly and I were in our pyjamas and dressing gowns. Grandpa looked tired. His short, stubbly hair seemed whiter than ever, his ruddy face pale.

'There's nothing to worry about,' he said. 'If it wasn't so late in the day they'd have let us bring her home.'

'I'll collect her in the morning,' Auntie Gwen said. She took Holly off to sleep in her bed with her that night.

I have very rarely suffered from insomnia. That night, however, I awoke at one-fourteen a.m., according to my illuminated watch. I lay there in my alcove, thinking about Grandpa, and whether this was to be his arduous ordeal for the rest of Grandma's life: fitfully shuttling between their home and Shrewsbury, often in the dead of night. I nurtured some vague hope of drifting back to sleep, but with each passing minute I knew that there was no avoiding climbing out and going downstairs, to empty my bladder and to fetch a glass of water for my parched throat.

Since I was heading for the kitchen anyway, I decided to use the downstairs lavatory rather than the bathroom at the end of the corridor on the first floor, so as not to disturb anyone. It meant disturbing the dogs, on the way through the pantry, but they only raised their heads and blinked drowsily at me, and went back to sleep. As I came stealthily back out into the hall, a shadowy figure passed silently a few yards ahead of me. It was a woman, dressed in pyjamas, whom I identified immediately as Aunt Lorna. I stood unbreathing and watched her climb the stairs.

The kitchen, with its many windows, took in just enough illumination from outside for me not to have to switch on a light. I had the uncanny impression that any noise I made inside would disturb nocturnal animals outside, whilst if, on the other hand, I was quiet I might be rewarded by the sight of a fox stalking around the yard, a badger loping across the lawn. I managed to open the cupboard and take down a glass without making a sound. Pouring the water was trickier, but I held the glass up close to the spout and at an angle, so that when I turned on the tap a fraction the thin trickle of water fell on to and slid down the glass side of the tumbler. I even drank slowly, swallowing carefully, so as not to make the slightest sound, my eyes peeled, staring outside. I placed the glass on the draining rack.

I could make out no movement in the darkness. Instead, I was disturbed by a creak in the room behind me, and turned: there was a figure emerging from the drawing room. It walked slowly through my grandparents' TV and sitting area, entered the kitchen, turned right towards the door giving on to the hall, and stopped. I could just about discern the person's head turning towards me, and I realised that, standing in front of the window, the light outside rendered my upper body in clearly apparent silhouette.

I was pretty certain that the figure was that of a ghost, probably, it seemed to me, that of Grandma's father – my own great-grandfather – who'd reluctantly sold the house to Grandpa. Perhaps his spirit just wouldn't let go. The strange thing was that I wasn't scared, or at least was able to hold my fear at arm's length for the moment.

'Is that you, Theo?' the person asked. It was not a ghost, but my own father.

I let out a long-held breath of relief. 'Yes,' I said.

'Bit early in the morning to be getting up, isn't it?' he said. 'Even for such an early bird as you.'

'What are you doing?' I asked.

'Who, me?' Dad said. 'Oh, I was lost, old chap. How about you? Are you okay?'

I told him I'd woken up with a dry mouth and was just helping myself to a glass of water. I didn't mention that I suspected it had been caused by a prolonged bout of kissing, with Holly, earlier that evening; nor did I question my father as to how he could have got lost in the house he'd grown up in. I was going to tell him that the coincidence of he and I both being up in the middle of the night was nothing, that actually three of us were. But then I figured he and Aunt Lorna had probably bumped into each other already.

'Heading back up?' he asked.

I walked over to him. 'Dad?' I said.

'Yes, Theo,' he said, his gentle voice calm, patient.

'It must be so awful for Grandpa,' I said.

'Yes, it must be,' my father agreed. He opened his arm and I leaned in against his shoulder, shedding years in the intimate darkness. 'Poor Pa,' he said. I wasn't a teenager any more as I sobbed against my father's chest, but a young boy, wandering, dizzied by the grief and the rapture of what he'd found in his way.

As we walked through the hall towards the stairs my father suddenly stopped and said, 'Good God. Will you look at that?'

We gazed out of the glass front door. Snow was falling, small, luminous flakes, drifting gently to the earth in the moonlight.

V

I

We were due to go home after lunch the next day, Saturday. My parents had some engagement back in Oxford that evening. I, however, had no wish to leave. I awoke before my cousins, despite the interruption to my rest during the night, yanked my clothes on and skipped downstairs, fully expecting to find the house hemmed in by deep drifts of snow, its occupants marooned. When I could see none out of the front door I assumed it must be some kind of optical illusion, and carried on still full of hope into the kitchen, where I stood at the window, dismayed, unable to believe my eyes: whatever snow had fallen in the dead of night had melted. There was not a trace of it, no single patch of white in the garden, on the stable roof, even on the summits of distant hills. It was as if snow had never fallen, was an illusion, some obscure mutual dream of my father's and mine. I could see no point in even mentioning it to anyone else. There then fell from the sky, however, another, immediate consolation: the great spotted woodpecker that had been reconnoitring the house these last days, and which I'd heard but not seen, now alighted upon one of the bird feeders right in front of the window. It nibbled assiduously for a few nervous, alert seconds, before flying away. It was an adult male, a patch of red on its nape amidst the splashes of black and white; more red on the undertail. I felt a firm hand on my shoulder.

'He came to see you before you left,' Grandpa said. 'Worth waiting for, Theo,' he added, in such a way as to suggest I'd somehow ordered it this way: planned the timing of the woodpecker's visit and my parents' schedule both, for which my grandfather was congratulating me.

At breakfast, Auntie Gwen and my mother persuaded Grandpa to stay at home and let them collect Grandma from the hospital, to spare him one at least of the many trips he'd have to make.

'Jockie will help you out, won't he, Pa?' my father asked.

'Assuredly so,' Grandpa replied.

An hour later the other children had taken their place in the generational rota of breakfast and were munching toast or cereal. My father was doing the washing-up from the previous sitting, Grandpa was taking care of something or other in his study, and I was through in the TV area, talking to the dogs. Sel rolled on to her back as an invitation to me to scratch her tummy, Leda tried to lick my face. They both knew, apparently through psychic communion, that we were soon to go for a walk. When I heard piano music, my first assumption was that my father had found a portable radio, tuned it to BBC Radio 3, and placed it on the window sill in front of the kitchen sink, to listen to as he washed the dishes, as he did at home in Oxford, but even before I raised my head I knew that what I could hear was not broadcast but live music; and it was coming from the drawing room. Neither did I need to look at my cousins eating their breakfast to know that it wasn't Sidney seated at the piano: what I could hear was as far from her clumsy punching of the keys as could be imagined. Rather, notes of a hypnotic beauty, being performed with the utmost delicacy and sensitivity, cascaded through the air like jewels made of sound.

I stood up and walked towards the drawing room. I'm not sure anyone in the kitchen had even noticed the piano playing. My mind raced with crazy possibilities as to the sight that awaited me: the piano tuner was here; Grandma allowed some local child prodigy to use her piano for practice in the same generous way she used to let them ride her horses; a musical burglar had broken in and been waylaid by the baby grand, been unable to resist stopping to play it.

I entered the room, with trepidation. Not because I expected to find a stranger, in truth, so much as because the music, and the playing of it, were so exquisite. I wouldn't have pretended to a great knowledge of music, but owing to my parents' tastes the classical repertoire had been a part of the background all my life. Yet I'd never heard anything so pure – yet oddly familiar – as this. Aunt Lorna was seated on the piano stool, her back straight, her chin up. Her head seemed to have lifted a little from her shoulders. She was reading sheet music, while her elegant fingers danced upon the keys of the piano.

I stood there for a moment, watching, before I found myself moving towards her, drawn by a power I had no will to resist. I approached at a diagonal, a forty-five degree angle to Aunt Lorna's line of vision, so that although her concentration, her absorption, was profound, she must have been aware of this person's movement. The ethereal notes of the music seemed to lift me off the ground; I had no sensation of my feet treading upon the carpet.

I'm not equipped to describe the music Aunt Lorna was playing. All I will say is that, in the space of no more than five romantic minutes, it summed up the ineffable possibilities of true love, as well as the impossibility of ever realising it. It suggested, moreover, love not only for one other human being, but for all those one loved; for this world we lived in; for life itself.

I reached Aunt Lorna and stood behind her right shoulder. She was playing the second of Granados' *Danzas españolas*, the so-called 'Oriental'. I understood, as she played, how much she suffered, living her life as she did with my crude Uncle Jonny and their diabolical twins. How such a sensitive woman was able to share a realm of such vulgarity was hard to imagine. I thought of Baz and Xan's hideous karaoke, and could have wept for my aunt.

When she'd finished, Lorna sat for a moment, still gazing at the sheet music, as if there were some extra item of information there visible only to someone who had just played the piece, an inaudible secret coda to that musical glimpse of divine truth.

'That was so beautiful,' I stammered, blushing, as Aunt Lorna got up. She showed no sign of surprise at my presence.

'Thank you, Theo,' she said, stroking my cheek, and left the room.

It was only after she'd gone that a dire thought occurred to me: that the twins were both brilliant musicians. How could they not be? And that they had decided – possibly in conference with their mother – not to perform at the recital so as not to upstage their cousins: Sidney, Holly and I, we three uncultured novices.

We walked straight up the lower flank of the hill, Grandpa stumping upwards with his head down, the dogs chasing scents in the dead bracken, Xan and Baz scrambling on ahead then halting, bent double, struggling to get their breath back, while the rest of us caught up and climbed past them. Then they'd overtake us again, yelling and panting and dashing after the dogs.

Aunt Lorna chatted with Sidney about her A levels. Uncle

Jonny had stayed behind to 'take care of some business'. I pictured him down in the yard with his alternating phones, in uncivil conversation with other men stepping outside of their family homes. My father, though, was with us, and he was talking with Holly. I think he preferred to listen, because we were climbing steadily and no one could accuse Dad of being the fittest of men. I'm not sure what they were discussing. Summer holidays, it sounded like.

I'd not had a chance to talk with Holly yet that morning, but even if I had I'd no idea what to say. Perhaps she did. When I first saw her, when she came into the kitchen for breakfast, my heart missed a beat. And yet I realised almost immediately that what I felt for my cousin was not desire, but gratitude. The wonderful hour we had spent in the wardrobe, making our first blind discoveries of physical contact, prepared us not for one another but for intimacy with certain others we had yet to meet. Each of us, it turned out, had given the other a generous gift, and we had no further obligations.

As we rose higher, so that undulating upland country spread out around and below us. After the stillness of those last days, today was blustery: clouds scudded across the sky; the sun gleamed, then faded in sudden spurts; patches of hills and valleys lit up, then faded away, as dark shadows chased swiftly across the countryside.

Our grandfather always claimed the dogs kept him hardy. They had to be exercised every day, 'and so do I'. He would push himself up from a chair with a grimace, and moved stiffly between rooms, his spine bent, his neck stiff. You could see that the skeleton of his frame was gradually seizing up. But once he got walking on the hill he just kept marching forward, dismissing the arthritic inconvenience of his ageing bones, and it was an effort to keep up.

We followed a grassy track over the shoulder of the hill, crossed a shelf of high ground on which sheep grazed for whatever sustenance they could glean from the winter grass. The dogs ignored them. Then we cut up through the heather and bilberries and made for the summit.

'Rain in the west,' Grandpa remarked, to no one in particular, the only words he uttered on the entire ascent.

Climbing – or walking uphill, I should say; I've not scaled a rockface in my life – is an incomparable experience, for our gaze across the landscape revealed by our exertions is itself altered by the oxygen greedily inhaled, given to our blood, carried to our brain. One's muscles testify to the achievement and the view is one's reward. We could see to the east a wide swathe of the western side of central England; west, the rugged uplands of central and southern Wales. To the south-east rose the Malvern Hills. To the north, beyond Wenlock Edge and the Long Mynd, stretched a broad plain interrupted only by the round blob of the Wrekin.

Grandpa was gazing north-west. 'On a clear day,' he said, 'you can see Cader Idris.'

Aunt Lorna asked where Offa's Dyke was from here, and Grandpa pointed down to a gulley between two hillocks below and to the west of us. Xan asked who this Dyke was. Baz made some crude, quick response, but Grandpa ignored him.

'At the end of the eighth century King Offa of Mercia,' he said, 'the most powerful of the Anglo-Saxon kingdoms in this country, before there was any unified rule, built the earthwork to protect the western limit of his kingdom.'

'Who from?' Holly asked.

It was blustery up on the top of the hill. We all had to lean in and concentrate to hear what another person said. People had cold ears, red faces.

'From the British, who'd withdrawn from the Anglo-Saxon invasions, and the Welsh who were there already, and absorbed these refugees into their forces.' Our grandfather turned to Baz and said, 'A law decreed that any Welshman found east of the Dyke should lose his right hand. And, if he trespassed again, his head.'

'Wow,' said Baz, impressed.

'I bet that stopped those Taffs,' said Xan.

'Of course it didn't,' Grandpa said. 'The Dyke wasn't enough. Nor were the castles of the Marcher Lords, thirty-two of them strung along the border. The Welsh swooped out of those Black Mountains over there in swift, marauding raids. Disputed land, all this,' Grandpa said. 'It was once, doubtless will be again some day. Come on. You all look like you're going to freeze up here.' And with that he set off back downhill, and the rest of us followed.

As we descended, finding myself off to one side of the rest of the party, my attention was caught by something below me, to the west: with the clouds shifting and skitting across the sky, and pools of sunlight forming and dissolving in the fields, there was something moving; gold or silver was flashing. I looked and saw a line of riders snaking in from the west, their armour shimmering, the metal in their horses' bridles glinting. Amazed, squinting my eyes in the sun I watched and saw their Celtic spears; their bows and arrows; great iron swords slung over their shoulders. There could have been no more than ten or a dozen. A small raiding party.

My family carried on without me, disappearing over the brow of the hill without a backward glance. I let them go, and stood waiting for the time-leaping Welsh guerrillas to come closer, curiosity outweighing my fear.

The riders followed a path towards me. Less than a hundred yards away the lead rider dropped into a dip. The others followed, until they'd all vanished, momentarily. Then the first one rose out of the hollow, no more than forty yards from me now. As they emerged, one after another, I saw that they had changed: were not warriors but young women, in thick coats and jackets, gloves, jodhpurs, riding boots. They came up the path, which veered away, and rode past me. I stood and watched them pass. It was striking that none of the riders were wearing riding helmets. As they reached the open heather moorland their single file disintegrated, they kicked their mounts and broke into a canter, their hair blowing in the wind.

I turned and ran downhill to catch up with the others.

2

I was the one who saw Auntie Gwen's lime-green Berlingo bumbling along the lane below us. 'Grandma's home!' I called out, and we quickened our pace down the track, our footsteps slipping on the soft turf, the dogs barking. The sun was shut out from the sky now, the colour of the landscape muted to sombre brown, green and grey.

The gate off the hill was only a few yards along the lane from the entrance to our grandparents' property. We came down the drive, then cut across past the back of the house, coming out from behind the conservatory just as my mother was helping Grandma out of the front passenger seat of Gwen's car. She stood, but ignored our party advancing across the patio. Instead, Grandma turned to lean against the roof of the car and watch what was happening over by the coach house: a tractor was parked there; connected to the back of it was the largest trailer I'd ever seen. It made the tractor look like one of those tugs that can tow a ship many times its size out of harbour. Another machine which was like a digger, with a great grabbing claw on the end of its hydraulic, retractable arm, lifted a rusting old plough, pulling it free from other wrecks with which it had become entangled, and dropped it into the giant trailer.

The noise was terrific: a cacophony of grinding engine and clanking, screeching, resounding metal. It was extraordinary that we'd not heard it as we came down off the hill, but I surmised that the blustery winds had carried the sound in the opposite direction, out into the wide valley below. Neither had we been able to see the activity, hidden by the coach house and by various trees in the hedge of the paddock above.

We stood in the yard, staring at this ghastly, impressive spectacle. One man stood on the running board of the tractor, leaning against his cab, a cigarette in the fingers of his trailing hand, watching his colleague operate the digger. Uncle Jonny stood with his back to us, watching the operation, hands on his hips.

My father started running in silence, his head low, gathering speed as he crossed the yard. Someone yelled, 'No!' – one of the women, I think, I couldn't tell who. Dad ignored her. Uncle Jonny clearly couldn't hear.

Perhaps he did hear my father's footsteps, or sensed his approach in some other way. I don't think so. I think he just happened to glance over his shoulder at that moment, that he'd been turning round every few minutes for some while now, hoping that these men he knew from childhood, and whom he'd recruited in the pub on Christmas Eve, would finish the job before we walkers, or Grandma, returned home.

Uncle Jonny turned his head as my father reached him, and took the full force of my father's lunge on his twisting spine. They both hit the ground. Jonny was immobilised, but Dad scrambled to his feet and leaped on his brother and began punching his head and face.

The tractor driver, lolling on the running board, was oblivious to what was happening a few yards behind him, but the digger driver must have been able to see, because he switched off the engine, opened the door of his cab and gesticulated at his colleague, pointing at the struggling men.

Auntie Gwen, meanwhile, led the dash across the yard from

our end, followed by Grandpa. Aunt Lorna and my mother remained rooted to the spot, as did we children.

The tractor driver, though paunchy and middle-aged, leapt nimbly down and rushed over, reaching my father at the same moment as Auntie Gwen, and together they pulled him off Uncle Jonny, who lay on his back on the ground. The dogs barked and jumped around them, excited, uncomprehending. Even from the distance at which we stood I could see Jonny's face was cut and bloodied, and, now that the machines were silent, I could hear him groaning.

'Okay,' my father said, in a hoarse, rasping voice. 'Okay.' But the tractor driver wouldn't let him go. The digger driver and Auntie Gwen were bent over Uncle Jonny.

A commotion behind me made me turn: Aunt Lorna was shepherding the twins towards the front door. I caught Holly's eye. We looked at each other, without expression. On the other side of me my mother was encouraging Grandma to turn away and head for the house as well. 'Theo,' she called to me.

I looked back across the yard. Grandpa told the tractor man to let my father go, and he obeyed. Grandpa put his hand on Dad's shoulder. 'It's all right, Rod,' he said. My father had started trembling, shocked by what he'd done; of what he was capable of. 'It's all right, son.'

'Theo!' Mum called again. I ran over and took my grandmother's other arm, and we escorted her across the patio towards the house.

3

Aunt Lorna drove the Land Cruiser, Uncle Jonny in the passenger seat, in the reclined position, his face swelling, the twins in the back. They were gone within the hour.

Grandpa had told the men to finish their job, and he paid them himself. Grandma went to bed. The rest of us ate a lunch of leftovers. No one had much to say. My father felt so bad about what he'd done he went back outside, and the dogs had a second walk under the dark, glowering sky. There were no more clouds, only a huge blackening bruise moving in over the border from the Welsh mountains.

In the afternoon, we drove home through the rain. Auntie Gwen had decided to stay through the New Year, up until the girls had to go back to school. Melony, it seemed, was prepared to come back.

When Holly and I hugged farewell, we did so without awkwardness. I felt the fullness of her body in my embrace, smelled the skin of her neck.

'Good luck,' she whispered.

'You too,' I said.

'I'm always there if you need me,' she said, which was the sweetest way of saying goodbye I've ever heard. I knew she would be. We were related, after all.

'Me too,' I said.

The wipers laboured to and fro across the windscreen, clearing, along with the headlights, the way ahead, water washing against the glass, splashing off the tarmac. I read my book from Grandpa, *The Stories of the Greeks*, with surprised relief as it became apparent that I could do so without an old familiar nausea rising from my stomach, and then with deepening absorption, introduced in the stories of Pyramus and Thisbe, of Daedalus and Icarus, to a further – epic – dimension to our stories.

In the front, hands on the steering wheel, plasters on his knuckles, my father drove steadily, past Bridgnorth, cutting across country to the M5, and along and down the other motorways home. Neither he nor my mother beside him said a word, until we'd come off the M40 and were on the A34 to Oxford.

'It's the strangest thing, Amy,' he said. I suspect he'd forgotten I was there, in the back of the car; at the rear of their lives. 'I've wanted to do that all my life. Ever since the little bastard invaded our family when I was five years old. And now that I've done it, I feel like such a fool. You know? Just so, so stupid.'

I could see my Mum's right hand. She placed it on Dad's thigh. 'You're a man, Rod,' was all she said. I could hear no intonation in her voice. Did she mean he was a human; or a foolish male; or a hero? To this day I don't know what she meant.

Our grandmother died the following March. She had refused ever to leave the house again and go into hospital. A bed was brought into the drawing room, and a rota of nurses were on hand. But Grandpa couldn't bear to watch her suffering as the disease grew worse, and when she became unaware of her surroundings he had her taken into the hospice in Shrewsbury, whose doctors and nurses administered sophisticated medication that eased her ordeal: she lapsed into a coma, my mother assured me, and slipped away.

We returned, all of us, to attend our grandmother's funeral. In such circumstances, and with our behaviour as constrained as the mourning clothes we wore, my relatives appeared odd to me. It was as if we'd come back together for the purpose of performing a coda to the drama of that Christmas. We played our parts, burying Grandma in her family plot in the small churchyard, then left.

That summer I was invited to join a schoolfriend's family on their holiday abroad, and I accompanied my father on only one weekend visit to the Shropshire hills. The garden was flourishing, tended by a new gardener after Jockie's retirement, and the house was clean and tidy: Bronwen came in every day, and cooked meals which she left for Grandpa with precise heating instructions written on notes stuck to the dishes. But the dogs greeted us with a strange restraint when we arrived, and plodded about the house with Grandpa, flopping on the carpet beside his chair. He admitted that he rarely took them on the hill, so I spent hours with them, running in great loops around the valley, improving my fitness for the team I'd joined at Norham Gardens Tennis Club.

Back at the house, Dad asked Grandpa how his history book was coming along, and tried to encourage him.

'If there's any research you need to do, you know, you could always come and stay with us,' he said. 'I could get you a visiting reader's ticket for the Bodleian.'

Grandpa sucked on his pipe, and gazed out of the window.

'Not much point now, old son,' he said.

In the autumn Grandpa took the dogs, Leda and Sel, to the summer house, and shot them. He then turned the gun on himself. He left no suicide note. Had layers of sadness, or disgust, built up in his soul? The loss of his orchards, life without his beloved, conflict between his children. The deeds to the house had been handed over in lieu of interest on a loan, with Grandpa given one year in which to leave. I don't know. He had reinvented himself once. He couldn't do it again.

After his funeral my mother and I came back to Oxford. My father, Auntie Gwen and Uncle Jonny remained at the house for some days, conferring with solicitors, estate agents and auctioneers, and wrangling with each other. Uncle Jonny promised he'd build his business up again, and pay them their due share of the house value one day.

The contents of the house had now to be divided. When Dad returned I asked him about Grandma's crazy idea to put coloured stickers on the furniture, and he said he thought the stickers were a grand idea, which would have worked well. In the event, Uncle Jonny had the sense to withdraw from the 'division of spoils', as my father put it. Dad let Gwen choose what she wanted. He and Mum took a desk of drawers. The rest was auctioned off. I told him how sad I thought that was, that Grandma had tried so hard to ensure things worked out after she and Grandpa were gone.

Dad told me not to be downcast. 'Harmony exists only in music, Theo,' he said. 'And then rarely. A single family can no more sort out its legacy than society can,' he said.

He also informed us that Grandpa had bequeathed me his library – and his desk, at which I type this now. What remains of his books surrounds me, scattered now on the shelves. I remembered the story, which Grandpa had first told me, of the library of Leofric, a Cornishman who was educated in Lotharingen in the Rhineland, and returned to England in the early ten-forties in the entourage of Edward the Confessor. Anointed Bishop of Exeter, he had a new cathedral built, the one that stands there to this day, and established his library. In that library there survived a verse collection, known as the Exeter Book, that is one of the principal sources of knowledge of Anglo-Saxon poetry.

I never did ask my father what he was doing with my beautiful Aunt Lorna that Boxing Day night. Did something take place between them? My parents' marriage was the most companionable I've known, but did it offer either of them every shade of happiness? What marriage ever can?

What he could give Aunt Lorna is less obvious. A shoulder to lean on, someone to listen to her tell him that the dynamic man she had married had lost his power for her. That's what I suspect to be the prosaic fact, and I'd rather let my imagination loose a little. For I am my father's son, and I feel no disloyalty to my mother's memory to wish for him to have kissed a woman such as Lorna.

As you yourself may know if you're reading this, books need to be treated properly if they're to burn well. If you toss them on a fire, the outer edges char, but little else. You have first to rip off the covers – which, if a decent hardback, can be torn up and used for kindling – and then soak the bulk, returning it to pulp, before pressing it tight as it dries. That way you get a solid, quasi-wooden brick that burns as slowly as peat.

I select which books to burn. Once I had accepted the necessity of so doing – which a cold house in winter made easy – the process has been one of increasing difficulty, and weighed heavily on the heart. Recently, precious volumes have been burned. The only consolation – if I can call it that, which I can't, really; it is more a distraction – is the notion that I am discarding superfluous books as I work my way towards an essential library. Which, ultimately, will be those precious books that I would rather pass on intact to my own grandchildren than use to stop them shivering, their teeth chattering. Does that make sense? Perhaps, soon enough, we shall discover there are none.

The passage of time renders all things strange, corrupted, enticing, in memories in one's mind as with the objects of material existence. It's natural that that period of one's life, launching out of childhood, on the threshold of adulthood, of – as one imagines it to be – true life; it's natural that this period of hope, and of potential, should be looked back upon as one of innocence. I understand this. Now, of course, with what has happened since, we're well aware that although the seeds of corruption had already been sown all around us, and were growing in this world, this planet, this mind of God, it really was such a time. That Christmas of fifty years ago.

My children blame their parents – as I did mine, and no doubt they did theirs, and so on, back to time immemorial. But the fact is, Grandma was right: What have I done? Did I do enough? Clearly not. None of us did, did we? It would have been better to have taken a chance – for the thinkers to turn into doers – to have betrayed ourselves and become men of action, flawed heroes of our own lives. Who knows what might have happened?

ACKNOWLEDGEMENTS

Special thanks to my mother and stepfather, Jill and Hugh Scurfield, in whose part of the world, in south Shropshire, this novel is set; and with apologies to them and the rest of my family for the fact that all the characters in this novel are fictitious.

A particularly interesting and helpful book was *Shropshire Hill Country* by Vincent Waite.

Many thanks to Jason Arthur at William Heinemann, and Victoria Hobbs at A. M. Heath.